TAMPER

A NOVEL

BILL ECTRIC

billectric

Library of Congress Control Number: 2025915604

ISBN: 979-8-218-74484-7

Published by **billectric,** Jacksonville, FL

TAMPER

BILL ECTRIC

Published by billectric

FIC061000   FICTION / Magical Realism
FIC060000   FICTION / Humorous / Dark Humor
FIC009050   FICTION / Fantasy / Paranormal

Thanks to Steve Aylett, Dale R. Gowin, Paula King, Sonya King, James Morrow, Ed Champion, Judih Haggai, James Warnick, Mikael Covey, Karen Black, Michael Norris, Kris Saknussemm, Richard Toronto, and Levi Asher for feedback and/or proofreading.

For Roger Bolen

"While yet a boy I sought for ghosts, and sped
thro' many a listening chamber, cave, and ruin
And starlight wood, with fearful steps pursuing
Hopes of high talk with the departed dead."
- Percy Bysshe Shelley,
Hymn to Intellectual Beauty

Chapter One

1969

The Dome in the Woods

Rumors had persisted for years that a mysterious "dome" stood somewhere in the woods about two miles west of my hometown, Hansburg, Virginia. We heard it was used by witches for naked ceremonies, or as a Civil Defense Radar Station, or drinking, and one story said that words appeared and disappeared on the walls, and in freezing weather, a colorful magnetic aura hovered over the dome. Roger thought it should be *aurora*, not *aura*, so when I wrote about it in the high school paper, I slipped both words into the story.

Winter, 1969, tenth grade. We had a heavy winter blizzard. Snow and ice on steep, hilly roads can make driving dangerous. Hopefully they would close the schools. I woke up to the high-volume blare of Crosby, Stills, and Nash on my radio-alarm clock. Through open curtains I saw a deep snow drift, covering the back yard. The snow was high as my window, bright and clean in the gentle morning light.

Throwing on my robe, I walked through the living room to the kitchen. My mother sat with her coffee and toast, listening to her radio. The same song by Crosby,

Stills, & Nash playing at mom's lower volume sounded smooth and melodic.

"You're just in time," she said.

The radio DJ broke in as the music faded, "We have an update on school closings. Montgomery County, which includes Hansburg, Blue Meadows, and . . ."

The phone rang. It was Roger.

"Did you hear?" he asked.

"Today is a perfect day to look for the dome."

The Highway Department had recently completed Interstate 81, which runs North and South, a quarter mile west of Hansburg. Roger and I decided to walk, in the snow, across the Interstate, into the woods, in search of the dome.

"Or magic mushrooms," said Roger. "Meg Longino says cold weather puts magic mushrooms into fruiting condition."

We didn't have drivers' licenses, just learner's permits and we didn't want a parent along.

The previous summer, our friend Paul Clemens had drawn a topographic map for Boy Scouts. He won a badge for accuracy. On the map, Interstate 81 incorporates part of **County Road 114,** until **Old County Road 114** turns left and follows a rectangular route through the woods and then reconnects with Interstate 81. Paul Clemens labeled the rectangle "4 Corners." But Paul disappeared along with his map the following Fall. He became a missing person. Now it was Winter and neither the Police nor anyone else had found him. We told the police about "4 Corners" but they said it didn't exist.

Roger and I trudged up the street, our breath visible in the cold air. The only sound was the occasional pristine crackle of tree branches, snapping from the weight of icicles. I pulled the furry flaps down from my winter-style ball-cap, to keep my ears warm. Roger was tall, almost six-nine. He wore a brown police-issue fur-lined jacket and a police-issue State Trooper Stetson hat. His father had given him the hat and jacket after resigning from the State Highway Patrol to become the Hansburg City Jailer. Roger pinned a metal Smokey the Bear badge on the front of his hat.

He also had a police-issue leather cartridge pouch attached to his belt. No ammo included. Today he opened the pouch to reveal a compass, a pocketknife, two candy bars, a Zippo lighter, a joint, and two knotty cheroots, or as we called them, Clint Eastwood cigars, like the ones Eastwood smoked in *The Good, the Bad, and the Ugly*. Roger filled me in on his plan.

"At the end of this street, we have to cut through some people's yard, between two houses in a cul-de-sac, and over their back yard fence, and we'll have to do it fast. Or just ask permission. After the fence, we walk through a field to the Interstate Highway."

Leaving footprints in the snow between the last two houses in the cul-de-sac, we walked into someone's back yard without permission. A tall wooden fence ran along the rear property line. Roger interlocked his gloved fingers, palms up, and said, "Step up."

He boosted me over the fence and somehow boosted himself over.

"It's called climbing," he said.

On the other side of the fence, a large meadow stretched out before us. The deep snowdrift against the fence made walking difficult at first. Further into the field, the snow levelled out until our boots crunched into a thin layer of frozen grass that glinted in the sun. After fifteen minutes, we could see a barbed wire fence, and beyond that, a tractor-trailer cab gliding along the horizon.

"That's the Interstate," said Roger.

It started snowing again. We smoked the joint. The gleaming white field seemed vast. The air felt magic.

We ran across the northbound stretch of Interstate 81. It's a lot wider than it looks when you're driving. We finally reached the median and walked to the southbound stretch of road. Roger was looking into his cartridge pouch when I said, "Let's go."

"Oh -kay… no wait…"

But he was too late. I ran onto the asphalt. But like a dumb-ass, I was looking south for oncoming traffic and saw none because this was a southbound lane and the car was behind me. A loud shriek of brakes jarred me out of my skin.

The wide chrome grill of a metallic-green '68 Chevy Bel Air would certainly have struck me dead had the driver not hit the brakes and swerved onto the median. The big sleek Chevy rumbled to a stop a few yards past Roger as he took long backward strides to get out of the way, one hand on top of his trooper hat, to keep it on.

I ran to the median and walked toward the car. The driver rolled down her window and I recognized Anne Wade, who was in our drama class.

Anne said in rigid, measured tones, "Oh – my – God!"

"Sorry," I said, stepping closer to the car to face Anne's wrath and reproach.

She said, "Did you not even look? Were you trying to die?"

With her long blonde hair, vogue sunglasses, and winter scarf, Anne looked like a movie star. But my eyes moved quickly to the girl in the passenger seat, Nancy Griffin. She wore a light blue knitted wool cap, embroidered with white deer, and her silky black hair curved inward symmetrically around her neck.

Roger tapped on Nancy's window. She rolled it down.

"Hi, ladies," said Roger cheerfully, leaning into Nancy's window. "You okay, Anne?"

I spoke across Anne, to Nancy, "We're looking for the dome!"

Nancy said, "I remember you telling me about it, Whit. Do you think it's really out there?"

"Well," I said, "we vetted a kid whose older brother saw it."

Anne said, "Why don't you guys swap windows instead of yelling over me?"

Roger said, "Why don't you girls come with us to look for the dome?"

"I can't just leave the car here," said Anne.

"It'll be okay," said Roger. "Park it over there, closer to the woods."

"Why didn't you do it?" said Anne. "It's cold."

Nancy said, "Come one, Anne, let's do it. It'll be fun!"

"Alright," said Anne. "But we can't be gone long."

After parking the car, Anne put on a pair of gloves, pulled her scarf around her neck and threw the strap of a handbag across her shoulder. Nancy put her hands into the pockets of her blue herringbone wool coat and smiled at me. Roger checked his compass again, and the four of us headed into the woods. Roger lit one of the cheroots.

"What is that?" asked Anne.

"Clint Eastwood cigar," Roger said through his teeth, biting the cheroot.

"I want to try it," said Anne.

Roger looked sideways, pretending like he was deciding if he should let her smoke. She reached up and took the cigar from his mouth. She giggled with pursed lips as she took a drag of the cheroot. He handed me the other cigar and lit it for me with the Zippo. We walked and talked.

A quarter mile into the woods we emerged into an expansive snow-white clearing. Some crows flew overhead. Gray mountains elevated the distant western skyline. There was a small, deserted old farmhouse, some pieces of wood and concrete on the ground, and by God — a big metal dome! It was about fifteen feet high and fifteen feet wide. Patches of copper colored metal glinted through a thin layer of snow.

"Wow," said Roger quietly.

"Extraterrestrial," I said.

"It's a silo top!" said Nancy. "This used to be a grain silo made of concrete, with a wooden frame and a metal top. It collapsed."

"Probably from old age," I said.

"Maybe" said Nancy, "then too, under certain conditions, a spark can ignite grain dust to explode inside a silo."

Roger found the door-sized entrance that someone had cut in the dome. He had to lean over to get through. Anne followed him in.

I said to Nancy, "Silos can blow up?"

"Yeah, weird, right?"

We followed Roger and Anne into the snow-brushed copper dome. Red paint coated the inside walls. From above, a soft column of light diffused outward from a hole in the center of the top.

Roger and I scanned the walls, walking the entire circumference of the round room in opposite circles, passing each other at one point.

"I don't see any writing," I said.

"Me, either."

"What are you looking for?" asked Nancy.

"There is supposed to be ghostly writing on the walls," said Roger.

"Says who?" asked Anne incredulously.

"We can't reveal a source."

There was enough light for any writing on the wall to be visible, but we saw none.

"What do you mean by ghostly?" asked Anne.

"Is it all squiggly?" asked Nancy, wiggling her fingers up at Roger.

"We may never know," he said.

We turned our attention to a half dozen old dried-up paint cans on the floor next to the wall. Two empty whisky bottles lay next to the paint cans.

"We should have brought whiskey," I said, tapping one of the empty bottles with the toe of my wet rubber boot.

"These buckets had blue, yellow, and red," observed Nancy, "but the wall is nothing but red."

"Well," said Anne, reaching into her handbag. "Look what I've got here."

She pulled out a flask-shaped bottle of 90 proof peach brandy.

"I could kiss you!" said Roger, which he did.

We passed the brandy around and Anne said, "I'm not cold anymore."

"Next time, I'm bringing a radio," said Roger.

I felt a golden glow of happiness inside. I walked along the curve of the red dome with one hand touching the wall, and said loudly, "A stately pleasure dome decree!"

"What?" said Anne.

"It's from Kubla Kahn," I said, still walking. "A poem by Samuel Taylor Coleridge. 'In Xanadu did Kubla Khan a stately pleasure dome decree!'"

Roger said, "Whit knows his shit! He'll be a top-notch writer someday. Other people have found the dome, but he'll be the first to write about it." He sipped from the bottle.

Anne screamed, causing Roger to spill brandy down his chin. She pointed to a section of the wall where words were literally appearing over the doorway. Even as we watched, the words got more solid and well-defined. They said:

4 WINDS PAUL CLEMENS

"Oh my God," said Anne. Her voice quivered. "Let's go. I want to leave."

Roger took a couple of clumsy steps and I saw that Anne was standing on the tops of his boots with her arms around him.

I looked at Nancy. Her face was radiant with wonder.

"The sun," said Nancy. "It's the angle of the sun."

Through the doorway, in the distance, we could see the sun going down behind the western mountains.

Roger said, "I see it." He handed me the bottle and put both arms around Anne, holding her close.

"Nancy," I said. "I think you're right."

Paul Clemens, or somebody, had carved words into several layers of dried paint. Later, someone painted over the whole thing with red. When the sun was high in the sky, the words blended with the same red paint that covered the rest of the dome's interior. But when the setting sun cast its light sideways through the doorway, it caught the rough raised edges of the carved letters, just enough to cast a thin shadow. This shadow formed the outline of the ghostly words.

"That's pretty amazing," said Roger.

"That scared the shit out of me!" said Anne.

"Me, too," I laughed.

"It's ghostly enough for me," said Nancy. "It's a real-life miracle." He dad was a preacher.

Anne said, "I need to get back to my car."

"We've completed our mission," declared Roger. "Let's go home."

Back at the car, Roger climbed into the front passenger seat beside Anne.

In the back seat, Nancy said, "I'm cold" and leaned on me.

I put my arms around her. She pulled off the springy wool hat and laid her head on my chest, just under my chin. Her black hair, mussed by the hat, smelled delicious. Before I knew it, my nose and mouth were touching her hair. Nancy raised her face to mine with her eyes closed and we kissed. We didn't stop kissing until the metallic green Chevy Bel Air pulled up to her house to drop her off.

Chapter Two

1972
The Astral Beat

The photograph showed a procession of ghostly orbs floating out of a dark room toward the camera.

One explanation for the glowing spheres is that dust particles, stirred by my presence, had reflected the bright flash from the camera, causing an optical illusion. Roger and I didn't accept that any more than we believed a few scraps of aluminum weather balloon could account for the many eye-witness stories about the UFO crash at Roswell, New Mexico in 1947. As far as we were concerned, this photo was going into our newspaper, *The Astral Beat*, as a ghostly manifestation.

I had taken the photographs with my 35mm camera in the pitch-dark basement of an old, abandoned church. In the summer of 1972, a few days after graduating from high school, I entered the church through a side door, stepped over some disassembled pews where a stack of them had toppled over.

Extinguishing my flashlight, I aimed at nothing and clicked the shutter a few times, each flash illuminating a desolate array of dusty angular junk. After developing the film, we were amazed to see spectral orbs of light floating in the church basement. I thought we should call them *orbs*, Roger liked *spheres*.

Roger and I were enthusiastic fans of anything involving unexplained mysteries. This was before the actual television shows, *Unexplained Mysteries*, *Ghost Hunters*, or *In Search Of.* There were plenty of books and magazines on the subject but reading other people's stories was not enough for us. We wanted to be a part of it.

We proclaimed ourselves investigators of the paranormal. Our friends Anne and Nancy proclaimed us goofballs who somehow persuaded local businesses to buy ads in our self-published zine, *The Astral Beat.* The girls' ribbing did not phase our enthusiasm. We all had fun.

Roger was a natural born PR man. Six feet, nine inches tall, he played basketball in high school and boxed at the Policemen's Youth Center. If Roger thought someone had bad intent, he knew how to assert himself with an imposing stance and clenched fist, but most of the time he was friendly and articulate. He usually wore an open white buckskin vest, with western tassels, over various band logo T-shirts. Roger's girlfriend Anne, an aspiring hairstylist of the emerging scissor-cut school, sculpted his black hair into layers, a style called the shag, popular among rock stars that year.

"The shag haircut," said Anne, "was created by Paul McGregor for Jane Fonda's character in *Klute*."

Roger quickly added, "Rod Stewart has one."

Roger sold a full-page ad to Rock City Records & Tapes because the store manager, Meg Longino, was a hippie who had been at Woodstock, and she was into *New Age*. He asked her, "Remember, you told us about that Wicca commune in Roanoke? How local churches are harassing them for practicing witchcraft?"

"Yeah, man," said Meg, chin raised, eyes obscured by the ruby glint in her rectangular granny glasses. "Those Wicca folk have freedom of religion like anyone else! They observe the passage of *seasons*, man, like the cycles of the *harvest*, you know?"

"And," added Roger, "They have herbs and roots that heal sickness and bring visions. The big drug companies don't like that because they don't want people to learn about natural healing. My friend Whit, here, is writing a story on it."

"Fight the power," agreed Meg quietly but firmly. "Hell yeah, I'll buy an ad."

Roger later told Anne, "I think the haircut helped."

We developed a system of presenting supernatural phenomena that we called the "three-point construct." There always had to be at least three points. The ghostly orbs floating in the church basement are a good example. We looked up the history of the church to see if we could dig up any dirt.

According to the archives at the public library, the abandoned Gothic structure had once been Grace Lutheran Church, but the Lutherans built a bigger, more modern facility, and sold the old church to the city. Some people wanted to tear it down and build a parking garage for City Hall. Others voted to preserve the church as a historical landmark due to its 19th Century Gothic architecture, with the steeples, stone archways, and bell tower.

We scanned the obituaries for people who had died under the Church's tenure. A man named Crebnor Miles had died from tuberculosis in 1912 at the age of forty. The wife, son, and daughter that survived him held a memorial service at Grace Lutheran Church, where they were members.

We looked up the church in an old book about our small town, called *A History of Hansburg, Virginia*.

"This is perfect!" said Roger in a loud whisper. "Look."

Back in 1910, the book said, a fire destroyed several buildings and apartments in the downtown area. The Lutheran church didn't burn, so it provided temporary shelter to all the people who lost their homes to the fire. Neighbors donated clothing, blankets, pillows, and food. The assemblage soon discovered that one man among them had tuberculosis. Fearing that his wife and children might also be infected, they quarantined the whole family in the basement of the church. Could that man have been Crebnor Miles?

"He didn't die until 1912," I said.

"My grandmother said some people live a long time with TB."

We had our three-point construct. If anyone questioned the connection between Crebnor Miles and the Lutheran church, we had (1) the obituary, officially documenting his memorial service at said place of worship. If anyone doubted that people had ever been (2) quarantined in the church basement, we had a record of that. While there was no record that Crebnor Miles had been among that group, or for that matter, that anyone died in the church basement, I had (3) a photograph of disembodied spirits floating in that very place!

"I have a good feeling about this one," I said.

"Me too," Roger agreed. "What we need is a quote. We need to visit Old Baxter."

Old Baxter lived down a dirt road, in a 1946 Airfloat Travel Trailer under a chestnut tree, surrounded by wildflowers. The trailer looked like a 1940s idea of a space-age moon rover. The front forward curve of convex observation window with silver trim.

Baxter usually needed a couple of dollars for some tonic.

"I mix it with sassafras root for my arthritis."

We gave Baxter enough money to get two bottles of whiskey, one for him and one for us.

"You boys can wait in the backyard," he said. "I'll be right back."

Behind the trailer, in the shade of the chestnut tree, we sat in decorative but corroded wrought iron chairs that must have looked good twenty years ago at some sidewalk café. Roger rested his arms on the round glass tabletop, rolling a joint. Insects buzzed in the honeysuckle-scented sunshine beyond our shaded nook. By the time Baxter returned from the liquor store, the buzzing had clicked into a symphony synchronized with the sparkling molecules around us.

Baxter emerged from the back door with a glass half-full of whiskey. He handed our bottle to Roger, who opened it, took a sip, and handed it to me.

"What do you boys want to know?" he asked.

"Do you remember something about people being put in the basement of the Lutheran Church after the big fire?"

"Oh, I know what you're talking about," said Baxter in a vague tone. "Yeah…I was just a little feller, but I'll never forget it."

"In 1912?" I asked.

"That's right," said Baxter. "I mean, I'll never forget my daddy telling about it. 'Course I was only, uh, let's see, not born yet, but yeah. Human beings herded into a cold stone basement like cattle. A terrible chapter in the history of Hansburg."

Chapter Three

1982
Archer House Skullduggery

Boat lights glimmer in the rippling water, sundown reflections on the Chesapeake Bay. A small boat docks softly in Hampton, Virginia near the University. Glenda Wells, Real Estate Agent, still wearing the smartly tailored blue business skirt and jacket and plastic nametag, disembarks, and takes a cab twelve miles inland into Olde Hampton. Ms. Wells uses her key to open the front door of the Olsen Archer House. She turns on the light, walks knowingly down the hall from the living room, into a wood-paneled writer's study. This was the study, office, and guest room of popular paranormal author Olsen Archer. The room displays mementos of the man's life and work. A collection of puzzle boxes from all over the world, books and journals, the requisite human skull, a small model of Stonehenge, framed art, (surrealism and pop art), and on the writer's desk, the classic 1972 IBM Selectric typewriter with a blue matte finish.

This room, and the rest of the house, had been the private property of Olsen Archer for twenty-five years, and tomorrow it would be open to the public as a landmark and museum, but in tonight's twilight, the house floats in limbo between those worlds. Glenda Wells is the real estate agent who arranged the sale of the house from paranormal investigator Olsen Archer to the Hampton Literary Society.

Straightening her blue business skirt and catching her breath, she strides purposefully across the carpet and sees some unfinished work. The outlet covers are still lying on the desk beside their screws. A couple of framed pictures are still sitting on the floor. Ms. Wells shrugs off a shiver and quickly locates a sliding door in the plywood wall paneling, behind the desk, just above the baseboard. She sits on the clean new carpet and slides the panel open, revealing some vertical pipes inside the wall. The pipes go up through holes drilled a board, but she taps the board and it swings down on a hinge. She reaches up inside and feels a thick envelope, or packet, taped to a pipe. Peeling it loose, she smiles at the idea that this packet and her real estate experience set the stage for a book on haunted houses, written by her.

Blowing strands of hair off her face with an upward puff, she leans forward to close the panel.

Like electricity, terror bristles through Glenda Wells from head to toe.

A face, deformed and inhuman, gazes up at her from the dark. Even more ghastly than the deformity is the silent shriek of unspeakable outrage, filling Ms. Wells with both revulsion and self-reproach, as though she were the intruder.

Her mind reels, processing disbelief into fear and panic.

She screams and runs out into the street. A car screeches to a halt. She collapses in the glare of headlights, her blue eye shadow washing down in tears.

The next day, when the Hampton Literary Society opened Olsen Archer's house to the public in Olde Hampton, Glenda Wells missed the ceremony. She was in the hospital suffering from exhaustion.

Roger and I were there the night it happened. We don't know what frightened her. It wasn't us. She scared *us* when she screamed and knocked over a chair to get outside. But we got what we came for. In her panic, Glenda Wells had dropped the long envelope. Roger snagged it.

Chapter Four

1960s
Treasure Hunt

I grew up in the grassy, rolling residential hills of a small town called Hansburg, Virginia. Some of my classmates lived on nearby farms. Located in the foothills of the Appalachian Mountains, Hansburg has some steep roads that make for splendid snow sledding in winter and hair-raising bicycle races in the summer. But like my parents said, it was all fun and games until the day my younger brother Jeff accidentally skidded sideways under a moving car.

It happened when Jeff was nine and I was thirteen. We lived in a modest white house at the top of Third Street, a street so steep and long we called it Danger Hill. Ten houses with lawns lined each side of Danger Hill from top to bottom. Jeff and I rolled our red Schwinn bicycles to the edge of Poplar, facing down the slope of Danger Hill. We had friends stationed at the side roads on the way down, watching for cars.

Jeff and I stood up on our bicycle pedals and lurched the top pedal forward and down when Lee blew the whistle. We pedaled hard, chains engaging sprockets oiled to pedal furiously, faster, until the downhill momentum probably carried us faster than our legs could pump. I was ahead of Jeff until my front tire hit a piece of gravel. My handlebars wobbled. I didn't wipe out, but it cost me some speed. Jeff bolted past me, leaning forward, hair blowing wildly. Our friends were diligent enough in halting vehicles that approached Danger Hill from the side roads, but none of us thought about someone backing out of a driveway. From the next-to-the-last house on the right, retiree Mort Fincham backed his black, whale-shaped 1948 Packard onto the road. Jeff's reactions reflected the lightning synapses in his brain. For a split second, he instinctively hit the back-pedal brake, but realized he was going too fast to stop in time. He tried to swerve around the front of the big car, but now the old man had stopped backing up, shifted into DRIVE, and commenced his forward turn. Jeff slammed on the brake, skidded sideways, and leaned away from the Packard. A trail of sparks followed the bike underneath the car as one pedal and both handlebar tips rasped against the asphalt. Jeff, his bicycle, and his shower of sparks slid under the car just behind the right front tire. Still advancing, the Packard's left rear tire pinned one of the bicycle rims to the ground. The trapped wheel became an axis, causing the rest of the bike to swing out on the opposite side of the car like a switchblade. It sent Jeff rolling.

Mort Fincham finally noticed something wasn't right. He stopped his car and got out. His mouth hung open and the glare on his eyeglasses gave him a vacant, lost expression. "He came out of nowhere!" bawled the old man. "I looked both ways! He came out of nowhere!" I rolled up beside Jeff, who was lying on his back, staring at the sky, but not moving.

Someone's mother stepped out on her front porch and shouted, "I called Hans Everly!" We didn't have 911 Emergency in Hansburg yet, but everybody in the neighborhood knew Hans Everly from the Rescue Squad. Soon, Hans and his crew were asking Jeff questions, like, "Can you move your toes? Do you know what day it is?" and shining a light into his eyes.

My parents arrived on the scene and scolded me bitterly. "Your brother looks up to you! Don't you know any better? Go home! We'll talk later!"

Dad picked up the mangled Schwinn and laid it in the back of his station wagon. "Clean up this mess first," he told me, indicating some wire spokes and plastic reflector shards that littered the skid area. Mom and dad got back in the station wagon and followed the Rescue vehicle up to the top of the street where my brother was released to our house.

I knelt to pick up the pieces. A lady in a bathrobe with freshly toweled hair came out of a cream-colored house on the left and said, "I'll help you with that." She wasn't wearing a bra. When she squatted beside me in that loose robe, I saw naked tits. They were an odd shape, I thought at the time. I want to say like, calabash, but I don't know fruit that well. "You're a handsome youngster," she said. "I don't know," I said glumly. We picked up the spokes and reflector pieces and dropped them in her garbage can next to her cream- colored house. I thanked her for her help and walked my bike up the street toward home. When I got to the top of Danger Hill, in front of my house, I turned right onto Poplar, where the pedaling was easier because the road was level. I rode all the way to the end of Poplar where Roger lived. We decided to stage a treasure hunt for Jeff and his two friends, Dennis and Bruce.

In the early sixties I dreamed I saw bones on the creek bank beside the road, at the bottom of Danger Hill. The next day I rode my bicycle to the creek and, sure enough, there was an old burlap sack, stained with dried blood, with some bones spilled halfway out of it. They turned out to be pig bones from the butcher shop, dropped accidentally on the way to the dumpster and maybe a dog dragged the sack to the creek bank. My dad said I must have already ridden past the bag of bones, earlier in the week, and it registered in my subconscious mind, so I dreamed about it. I didn't think so. It truly felt like precognition. "I believe you," Roger said when I told him about it in Drama class. "I remember when you sensed those leeches."

When our Drama teacher held auditions for a school play, she tried to cast Roger as a medieval executioner. Roger wanted the lead part. "You're so tall," said the drama teacher. "You would look so scary in that dark hood, holding that axe." My classmates and I listened to this, some of us sitting cross-legged on the stage and others in second row seats with feet up on the front row seat backs.

"Or . . ." I said, and no one seemed to notice, but when Roger looked at me, the other students and the teacher turned to look at me. "Donald Sutherland," I said, "broke the mold for you tall guys. At first, he could only get roles like the dumb guy in *The Dirty Dozen*, and the dumb guy in *Die! Die! My Darling!* Then he got the lead role in *MASH*, and I read that he's playing the lead in a detective movie called *Klute* with Jane Fonda."

"But who will play the executioner?" asked the teacher.

"Me," I said.

"A wimp executioner?" said Eric Littleton, stagehand. "The axe is almost as big as you!"

"Exactly," I said.

"I like it!" said Roger, and with a dramatic flourish of his hand toward me, he told the rest of the class, "This man understands theater!"

Roger and I did the treasure hunt for Jeff and his two pals, Dennis and Bruce. We left clues in and around stores along Main Street. One clue led to the next and if they got to the end, they found a small plastic skeleton in a bag, stuffed in a drain spout or sitting on a windowsill in back of the old city jail. Not much of a treasure, but they loved it. They asked us to do it again and again. We walked down Danger Hill (3rd Street). At the bottom of the hill we took the East road, alongside a creek with no name. When the creek's direction turned North, we jumped over it behind the Kroger grocery store. We ran through the parking lot, past the front of the store to Main Street.

We slowed to a walk on the sidewalk. Roger stretched one hand forward and announced, "The grand vista of downtown Hansburg."

He thought he was being satirical. It's a small town. But Main Street bustled with activity on Saturdays. Kids, families, farmers, bankers, teenage drivers heading opposite directions but stopping to talk, window to window. A cop smiles and motions for them to get moving. People shopped, conducted business, and socialized. We had favorite places to go, down one side of the street to the crosswalk and up the other side. The first stop on the right was the Palace Theatre, the only movie theater in town. We looked at the posters to see the coming attractions. This is where we saw so many of those British horror films made by Hammer Studios, starring Veronica Carlson, Christopher Lee, Peter Cushing, and Barbara Shelley, sometimes with brief nudity. And those Roger Corman "B" movies with titles taken from the works of Edgar Allen Poe – *The Oblong Box*, *The Raven*, *Masque of the Red Death* – which almost always starred Vincent Price and almost never had anything to do with what Poe wrote. Nudity too.

We wrote a clue for the treasure hunt on the back of an 8" X 10" lobby card, which was a picture on display for the movie *Horror of Dracula*. It showed Peter Cushing as Van Helsing, driving a stake through the heart of a girl vampire. Roger slid the lobby card out of its frame, I wrote a clue on the back of the picture, and he put it back in the frame. The girl sitting in the ticket booth was accustomed to our shenanigans. She rolled her eyes and went back to reading a magazine. One time when I was buying a ticket, she popped her gum and asked me, "What color inks is in ya pocket protecta today, honey?"

The clue we wrote on the back of the lobby card was "bear foot blaze," referring to the stuffed bear in front of Blaze Hardware, where we would leave another clue and so on like that.

We stopped at the crosswalk with a young mother holding a child's hand, an undertaker, and a dog. When the light changed, we crossed the street to Rose's Five & Ten. You could trace each phase of childhood by walking down the aisles of Rose's Five & Ten.

Starting at the far end of the store: Stuffed animals, kiddy blocks with colorful letters and animals, safe toys for toddlers.

In the next aisle we liked to pull the strings on a dozen See & Says with arrows pointed to different animals for a cacophony of "This is a duck, the duck Mooooo! Oink, Oink! The dog, Meow! Says…Cow says! Woof Woof Quack!"

Next aisle: marbles, rubber balls, tinker toys, LEGOS, and the Potato Heads. Followed by toy guns and play kitchens, BB guns and Easy-Bake ovens. Plastic model kits of cars, airplanes, monsters, and a skeleton with vital organs visible. Frisbees, in 1967, arrived in an array of psychedelic day-glow colors. We got tired of pogo sticks and went back to bicycles. I gravitated to a display table near the models. The items on this table were divided into someone's idea of boy and girl sections. On one side, pocketknives, wallets, and stopwatches. On the other side, sewing kits, handbags, heart-shaped pencil sharpeners, then colored pencils, and next to the pencils were those cool diaries with lock and key. There was a vague attitude among my friends and my parents that the diary was a girl's item, but I think it was just poor placement on the display table. Diaries came in Navy blue, cherry blossom pink, forest green, and Highland plaid. Which color will I get? I read a magazine called *Famous Monsters of Filmland*. I came to understand that the editor and publisher of *Famous Monsters* were making money writing about science fiction, horror, and fantasy. This legitimized my interest in writing and documenting weird things. I bought a green diary. I told my friends and parents "I'm writing an original science fiction screenplay and I don't want anyone to steal my ideas," thus it was locked.

Roger and I organized the last treasure hunt in the summer between our sophomore and junior years. We stopped going to Rose's Five and Ten. We went a block further down, across the street, to Rock City Records & Tapes, which opened with a much wider selection of psychedelic music. The owner of Rock City, Meg Longino, played the records for us before we bought them. She told us intriguing backstories of the pop stars, like Jimmy Page's interest in Aleister Crowley, the occultist. Page bought Aleister Crowley's house and bad things happened to the band.

We ventured past Rock City Records. Further along on the same side of the street were a Smoke Shop, Pawn Shop, the Army/Navy Recruiting Office, the entrance to a dark alley, an all-night diner and on to the Greyhound Bus station, and Main Street branched off into State Road 114 that carried traffic out of town and around to the Interstate.

Chapter Five
1978
The Psychiatrist

"You should stop blaming your parents for your quarrel with reality," said Dr. Carnes, casually.

He leaned back nimbly in his chair, hands behind his head, framed diplomas on the wall behind him. I thought he was going to prop his feet up on the desk. My psychiatrist looked to be thirty-something, not much older than me.

"I'm not blaming my parents," I said. "I'm just telling you what happened."

"Well, go on, then. You say your mother gave you the drug paregoric?"

I studied the pastel tan and light blue Aztec pattern in the arm of my comfortably stuffed chair. Nice texture.

"You know what paregoric is, right?" I asked, still looking down.

"They stopped making paregoric in the late fifties," Dr. Carnes answered correctly. "It was a medicine made from camphor and alcohol and opium. They used it mainly to treat diarrhea and as cough medicine."

"Very good," I said, looking at him. "Well, my mother says that when I was a baby, she used to rub paregoric on my gums when I was teething."

"Because it hurts when your teeth are coming in," the shrink interrupted.

"You should have become a pediatrician," I said sarcastically.

"Right now I feel like one," he shot back. "Do go on."

"Well," I said. "I remember lying in my crib, looking up at these pictures on my bedroom walls. Eight pictures, two on each wall. They were Snow White and the Seven Dwarfs. You know, Happy, Doc, Bashful, Sleepy…"

"Yes, I'm familiar with the dwarfs," said the shrink, a bit impatiently, I thought. "But you were very young. How do you remember this?"

Ignoring his question, I continued, "So I'm lying there, and the picture of Grumpy looked scary. He was scowling at me. His eyebrows bristled and writhed like wooly worms."

"Caterpillars?"

"And every time a caterpi - wooly worm fell to the ground, a new eyebrow grew, and then bristled into another caterpillar and fell again. And another one grew. I looked at Happy, and his red grin stretched wider and higher until the curve of his lips broke through his pink cheeks, splashing blood on the wall."

"But, Whit," the shrink tilted his head skeptically. "If you were teething, you were too young to even know what caterpillars were, much less paregoric."

"I knew caterpillars, chump."

"Sleeping in a crib?

"Maybe it was a small bed with a rail."

"What about the miners?"

"That was the first of many times I heard them. When I'd had enough of Grumpy and Happy, I turned my head and damn! two more horrid faces on *that* wall, so I closed my eyes, with my ear pressed against the pillow. I'm not saying they were miners, but that's what it reminded me of. Distant clanking like a coal car rolling on an ancient track, and pickaxes hitting earth and rock. And voices."

"What did they say?"

"I don't know. They were indistinct. I thought maybe the noises came from electric wires in the walls, but my dad said maybe it's your pulse near the eardrum. My mother said growing pains and hormones.

"One night the clunking woke me up and I saw someone in the dark at the foot of my bed."

"What did you do?"

"I closed my eyes. I thought it was a dream until something touched my crotch, and I opened my eyes and sat up. Then I stood up on the bed. It was pretty dark, but something like a big armadillo scuttled out of my room into the hallway. I heard the metal grate hit the floor."

"Metal Grate?"

"Yeah, our house was built with an oil furnace in the basement. The heat came up through a metal grate in the floor in the hallway. My parents got rid of the oil heater and put in electric heat with vents in every room. They covered the metal grate with plywood and a rug because they didn't need it anymore. To me it was like a secret passageway. The big oil heater was gone, so when my parents weren't home, Jeff and I would lift the plywood and grate and climb down into the dirt-floor basement of canning shelves and spider webs. I arranged my chemistry set on a table down there, away from prying eyes. The door to the back yard let me sneak out at night."

"What drugs were you on?" asked Dr. Carnes.

"Just antihistamine for the pollen."

"Tell me about your allergies."

"Well, when the pollen was bad, I stayed indoors and drew comic books at the kitchen table. Our kitchen had a Formica countertop, 1950's style, with squiggly designs in it, dark shades of green, red, and black. I could study those squiggles in a kind of reverie on antihistamines and saw faces and other things."

"I see shapes in clouds," said Dr. Carnes. "I don't need antihistamines for that."

"Everybody can see things in clouds. It's more intimate when faces emerge from the Formica in your home. It's like there is magic in that house."

"Is that why you are so interested in Richard Shaver's rock books?" asked Dr. Carnes.

Chapter Six

Rock Books

Primarily a science fiction writer of the 1940s, Richard Sharpe Shaver also created a kind of art he called "rock books." He cracked rocks in half and saw patterns in the exposed grain. He colored the patterns as he saw them with paint and ink, often resulting in weird scenes of lewd alien women and mythological humanoids. In doing this, Shaver claimed to be reading and interpreting "rock books" written by an ancient civilization.

He also claimed that fiendish underground creatures were "tampering" with his brain.

Shaver made his writing debut in a magazine called *Amazing Stories*. Created in 1926 by Hugo Gernsback, *Amazing Stories* is arguably the first science fiction magazine. In the 1940s, Richard Shaver sent a story to the magazine about a race of evil mutants, called Dero, who lived in underground caverns and sometimes captured humans to torture and eat. According to Shaver, aliens from another planet had abandoned these subterranean creatures on Earth, back in ancient times, and centuries of inbreeding underground had made them insane. Shaver also claimed that the Dero were using some kind of energy beam to send disturbing voices into his own mind. He called this mental harassment "tamper." The most remarkable thing about Shaver's entire body of work was his claim, in all apparent seriousness, that it was all true!

It was never clear whether Ray Palmer, the magazine's editor, believed that Shaver was serious, but *Amazing Stories* continued publishing Shaver stories because it increased their sales and thousands of letters poured in. Some of the letter writers claimed that they, too, heard strange voices in their heads. This annoyed the more serious science fiction fans, who looked upon the "Shaver Mystery" as a hoax.

Years later, in an interview, Editor Ray Palmer admitted that Shaver had spent some time in a mental institution. That made me like Shaver even more, because I had spent time in a mental institution, too.

As early as 1797, Bedlam patient James Tilly Matthews described the mental torments inflicted on him by the so-called "Air Loom," an early form of tamper.

Chapter Seven

1966

The Boy Who Hid in Leaves

Paul Clemens was the same age as me, twelve, but a year ahead in school. Intelligent, but not bookish, Paul showed us how to start a fire by condensing sunlight through a magnifying glass, and how to make a magnet with a nail wired to a battery. He gave us the idea to build motorless go-carts for downhill racing, made from wooden crates, with tires from old wagons and tricycles, steered with rope.

Paul was an outdoorsman. He hiked and climbed trees and his coarse brick-orange hair was only a couple of shades brighter than the tan on his seasoned, freckled face. His parents had home-schooled him while his father was stationed on Coast Guard Island near Oakland, California. When a back injury led to his dad to early retirement, Paul's family moved to Hansburg where his mother had grown up.

Green leaves were turning yellow, orange, red, brown, or spotty fungus. It was Autumn and chilly at night. We liked to play kick-the-can while the sun went down.

Kick-the-can is like a combination of hide-and-seek and tag. We played at Anne Wade's house because the back yard had good hiding places and her parents were nice. Anne was a lanky tomboy, back then, with short blond hair. Her yard had a large oak tree, two pine trees, a shed, a hedgerow of shrubs next to the house to crawl behind unseen, and this evening, three piles of raked leaves, gleaming wet from an afternoon rain.

Anne was "it."

"It" means she counted to fifty with her eyes covered. Everybody else hid and she had to look for them.

Anne found Nancy Griffin first.

She found me next. I sat on the ground beside Nancy Griffin, who looked like the pretty-eyed, dark-haired girl on the *Lost In Space* TV show, Penny Robinson, played by Angela Cartwright.

"Hey, Penny Raven Robinson."

"That's not anybody's name."

Nancy's silky black hair curved in around her face and the back of her neck. And there was something about her body. She wasn't overweight, but just plump enough that I wanted to squeeze her, to see how it felt.

I started quoting Poe's The Raven to her.

Anne shouted, "I see you behind that tree, Eric Littleton!" and Eric said, "Huh? Oh, I'm not even playing" and casually leaned on the tree.

Roger was behind the shed on a mission to free Nancy and me by kicking the can, but his head smacked into a power line that ran to a light on the corner of the shed. Sparks and smoke obscured the back yard for a brief time. During the shouting, Jeff ran out of nowhere and kicked the can, Anne's dad walked out the back door and caught the can without missing a beat. It was perfect.

"Watch that power line!" said her dad. "Don't even go near it or I'm quelching this jubilee."

Paul Clemens showed up doing handstands and we decided to start a new round of kick-the-can. But I had to take an antihistamine pill, so while the rest of the kids played, I knocked on the back door and asked Mrs. Wade for a drink of water.

Mrs. Wade invited me into the kitchen.

"I thought you only needed those pills in the spring and summer," she said.

"It's for chilblains."

I sipped the cold water and looked out the kitchen window at the kids in the back yard.

Roger was counting to fifty with his eyes covered. Every kid was so focused on hiding, they ignored each other. I'm the only one who saw Paul Clemens kneel beside a big pile of leaves, stick his hand and arm into the pile, and lift up. It seemed to me that by looking for tree branches in the pile, he leveraged the crisscrossing branches to lift a wider swatch of wet leaves, like opening a thatched roof. Paul rolled into that opening and let the leaves close on top of him. It all happened in a second. I later copied Paul's move.

Sundown.

Nancy was counting to fifty with her eyes covered.

Everybody scattered. I crouched beside a pile of leaves and reached my hand in. I looked up and saw Paul Clemens doing the same thing at another pile of leaves. He smiled his sunny crinkle smile and winked.

As a canopy of leaves fell on top of me, I caught sight of a plastic cylinder dropping near my left hand. I lay in darkness, not moving at first, but I could not resist tapping my hand around until it touched the cylinder, which turned out to be a flashlight with a plastic skull at the end that lights up, probably raked up by accident. Its weight told me it had batteries, but did they work? Yes, they did. The light came on. The skull glowed and grinned. I shut it off.

Under that half-decayed vegetation, I thought about the fortitude of hiding in leaves. Slipping into the leaves is only the beginning. The trick is to become one with the dank, earthy ground. To accept the musty closeness of dirt and crawling insects. It was almost like being intimate with death, or eternity, or with some knowledge on the edge of my mind that was simultaneously liberating and grimly harkening. It's why the skeleton grins, I think, and it's the last year I went trick-or-treating.

I felt something moving on my leg and lit the glow-skull near it. A green snake, maybe eighteen inches long, was gliding over my leg toward my right hand. I closed my hand when the snake glided over it. Hold it, don't choke it, I thought. The snake's tail whipped around as it tried to free itself and I was blowing my cover trying to hold it at arm's length above my body.

I heard Nancy's voice, as though far away, shouting, "There's a light in those leaves are moving!" She said it just like that.

I jumped up in an explosion of natty brown leaves and muck, snake in hand. Laughing hysterically, I chased Nancy Griffin around the yard with the snake. She shrieked and tried to use Anne Wade as a shield, holding Anne's arms from behind so Anne screamed and struggled to pry loose. Roger was laughing and Eric was yelling, "Stop it! Stop it!" which I think was directed at me.

Nancy was crying and suddenly I felt stupid. I dropped the snake behind the hedgerow where Jeff screamed and came out crying.

There was no sign of Paul Clemens. He never came out from under the leaves. Roger and I prodded the leaf piles with two rakes, mine turned backwards more like a poker. Eric kicked the leaves. Paul was not there.

The next evening Anne's father raked the three piles of leaves into one big pile and lit a magnificent bonfire. Everybody was there except Paul and no one had seen him. Yellow and orange tongues of fire danced high and warmed our faces. Eric said Paul Clemens was burned up, but we knew it couldn't be true. His parents reported him missing.

Roger and I went to Paul's house a couple of days later.

Paul's father came to the door in a robe and slippers, looking like he just woke up.

"Is Paul back?" I asked.

He shut the door in our face. We waited a minute. Roger said, "Maybe he's coming back." We finally left.

Sometime between Thanksgiving and Christmas, a For Sale sign appeared on their lawn.

The way Nancy Griffin told me on the phone was, "I closed my eyes and counted to fifty. When I opened my eyes, Paul was gone. The world knows Superman as the Man of Steel and Batman as the Dark Knight. Hansburg knows Paul Clemens as the Boy Who Hid in Leaves."

Chapter Eight

1980s
Fours, Whores, and Mustache Growers

"There were four of us who drove to the whorehouse district in old Jerez," I said, "and the address was 4 Alcázar!"

"Okay, stop" said Dr. Carnes. "The only thing in that statement I want to hear about is the whorehouse."

"As you wish. We'll get back to the other. We were in the Navy, stationed in Spain. These friends of mine figured out that I was lying about having had sex. They decided it was their duty to get me laid. Buddy Beckler, me, and two other guys piled into Buddy's rusty orange Volkswagen Squareback, a squat little station wagon, and drove to the whorehouse district in old Jerez."

"Was it seedy?"

"Actually, it was a beautiful, sunny day. Kind of hot, and Buddy's AC didn't work, so we had all the windows rolled down. The main street was lined on either side with orange trees and blue-flowered Jacarandas. We were flying high on Stil-2's, amphetamines, and had a cassette tape of Slade blasting hard rock music so loud, people on the side of the road were staring at the car.

"We stopped at a bodega for some chilled sherry. Oh, man, I'm not much of a wine or sherry drinker, but that Oloroso was delicious! It had a quenching, toasted fruit flavor and high alcohol content, too. I have a picture of us, in our sunglasses, laughing, sitting on the hood and roof of Buddy's Volkswagen, after we'd had a few drinks. Behind us, on the white stucco wall of the bodega, you can see tic-tac-toe strips of bright ceramic tile with those symmetrical fractal patterns, like ever-expanding mandalas of blue, green, yellow, and orange.

"From there, we drove a couple of blocks down a side street and parked in front of the bordello, a nice house with a courtyard. I followed my friends into the house, where a short, fat, middle-aged Spanish woman greeted us. She and Buddy carried on an amiable conversation in Spanish, and he handed her some money. I thought she was the Madame, you know, I thought she would introduce me to some young women to choose from. But she took me by the hand, led me into another room, and shed her dress in one quick shrug. It must have been some kind of a trick dress, I don't know.

"The first thing that caught my attention was the appendectomy scar on her flabby, hanging belly. She said something in Spanish, with a tone and expression that seemed friendly but businesslike. I think I smiled nervously. I didn't know if I was supposed to take off all my clothes, or just my pants, or just unzip my pants and whip it out.

"The prostitute made the decision for me. She motioned for me to sit on the edge of the bed, unzipped my fly, and put her head…down there, you know. I was nervous, and this was such an unnatural situation, I went limp. I couldn't get it up. I thought maybe I should tell her to lie down on the bed. Buddy had taught me how to say 'doggie style' in Spanish, but I wasn't sure if he was serious. I even started thinking maybe he had taught me to say something ridiculous, just to play a joke on me. I found out later that he had taught me the Spanish words for "butt fuck.""

"The woman said something in Spanish. It was like a mechanic saying, 'Well, you want to do this or not? I don't have all day.'

"All I could do is smile and shrugged, and said, 'Sorry.'

"The prostitute patted me on the head, said something in Spanish, and proceeded to scramble back into her dress. I was zipping up when she opened the door, my three friends were standing there, in high spirits, ready to congratulate me. The fat little woman held up one finger, smiled and winked at my friends, then curled her finger down slowly to indicate a dick going limp. I thought, damn, she didn't have to tell them!

"Buddy laughed and slapped me on the back, saying 'Ahhh, Whitley, don't let it bother you! You'll get it in the next time! Let's go have a drink!' Which we did."

"Amphetamines," said Dr. Carnes, "can increase your sex drive at first, but in the long run, they do just the opposite. Did you ever go back? To a prostitute?"

"No, I never made it back to a red light district. It turned out a lot of regular women are willing to have sex."

"Nancy?"

"She and I drifted apart."

"Where did you get the diet pills?"

"Off base. In Spain, the drugstores had some excellent diet pills you could buy right over the counter, no prescription, and they were top-class amphetamines. Anfetamina, por favor."

"That's one way to learn Spanish," said the shrink.

"The Navy told us not to buy them or bring them onto the base. They were legal for Spanish citizens but not us. But most of the druggists didn't ask questions. Just walk in and say, 'Una botella de stil-dos, por favor' and unless you looked like a speed freak, they'd sell it to you."

"Stil-dos?" asked Dr. Carnes. "Stil-Two?"

"Yeah, they were called Stil-2's. Stil-dos."

"And they sold them to you?"

"Oh, yeah, at first," I said. "After a while the druggist laughed and said, usted es demasiado flaco, un esqueleto! You're too thin! A skeleton!"

"So what did you do, then?"

"I got this friend of mine, Buddy Beckler, to go in and buy them. He was a big guy, kind of fat, spoke Spanish better than me. He never had any problem getting them. He used them, too. Jim the Corpsman used them but he wouldn't buy them for anybody else because the hospital's commanding officer warned that it was a felony. He didn't want to get in trouble if somebody wigged out or got killed."

"Tell me about Jim the Corpsman."

"Well, he was a hospital corpsman who was stationed at the base hospital. Looked like a lanky teenager trying to grow a mustache, but older than he looked, of course. Very intelligent. He loaned me a book about LSD called *The Electric Kool-Aid Acid Test* by Tom Wolfe."

"Ahhh, a hippie in the Navy," said Dr. Carnes. "I hope to God he wasn't on LSD when he was treating patients."

"No," I said. "I wouldn't think so, no. He never gave me drugs. He found out I was taking amphetamines, so he advised me on getting proper nutrition, drinking orange juice and milk. We smoked a lot of hash. It was so cheap over there!"

"Hashish?"

"Yeah, people brought it over from Morocco and it was like, a dollar for a gram!"

"We're getting a little off the subject," said Dr. Carnes. "I hate to stymie your enthusiasm for mind expansion, but why did you join the Navy in the first place?"

"Oh, man," I said. "That was such a spur-of-the-moment thing. I can't believe we did it. Up to that time, we mostly identified with the anti-war crowd, the hippies and protesters. Roger came up with the idea when he found out Anne was pregnant."

"By him?"

"No, by the seven dwarfs," I said snidely. "Of course, by him. That's why he wanted to join. See, one day when we walked to town, he says, 'I got something to tell you . . .Anne's pregnant.' I was like, 'No way! What are you gonna do?' And Roger said, 'Well, we're not sure if we should get married, but we definitely want to have the baby.'

"About that time," I continued, "We were walking past the Navy recruiter's office. Roger stopped right there and said, 'let's join the Navy before we get drafted into the Army! We can get the hell out of Hansburg! You can go to Navy Journalism School, and I can be an electrician.'"

Dr. Carnes asked, "Weren't you afraid of going to Nam?"

"The recruiter told us that the Viet Nam war was winding down and troops were being withdrawn. Which was true. The war ended while I was in Spain."

"Where was Roger stationed?"

"He ended up in the Army!" I laughed. "It turned out he was too tall for the Navy. Six foot nine! The Navy has a height limit, so he went into the Army instead. He ended up stationed in Germany as an MP."

"Military Police," mused Doctor Carnes. "Wasn't his dad a cop?"

"Yeah," I smiled. "Roger always said he'd never be a cop and he ended up as an MP in Germany for two and a half years. He got written up once for growing his mustache too long. I got kicked out of Navy Journalism school for some tomfoolery."

"Because that diary kept you up all night," said the shrink. "That's my understanding, anyway."

"Yeah!" I said. "Yeah, trying to remember all the configurations, like, you know, it's not meaningless."

"But on every page, you obsess on the number four."

I looked at the Aztec pattern in the arm of my chair.

He looked at me quietly for a moment and changed the subject, saying, "How can you compare the creator of Sherlock Holmes to that hack Richard Shaver?"

"Call Shaver a hack if want, but he got published," I said.

"You would like to be published, wouldn't you?"

"I've been published," I said. "I had my own newspaper."

"Yes, I know," said Carnes. "Your paper's circulation was a small segment of a very small town."

"It's all relative."

"I suppose so," said the shrink nonchalantly. "I've been published of course, but I don't make a big deal of it."

"Of course not," I said.

"Yes," he continued, "*The American Journal of Psychology, Mental Health Quarterly, Psychiatric Counseling Journal*, you might appreciate my paper on the *Search for Meaning in Inanimate Objects*," and reaching into the bottom drawer of his desk, "I think I have . . . why are you looking at me like that?"

"Oh, don't mind me," I said. "Do go on with your book report."

"No, you're right." He closed the drawer and leaned back again. "It's a bit technical, anyway."

"I'm right about what?"

"Let's get back on track," said Dr. Carnes. "You have an appreciation for both Doyle and Shaver, and that's perfectly alright."

I looked up from the tan and turquois pattern in the chair.

"Doyle and Shaver both believed in unseen worlds," I said, "and people scoffed at them for their beliefs."

"What unseen world did Conan Doyle believe in?" asked the shrink. "I would think the creator of Sherlock would value facts and . . . wait a minute, are you talking about *The Lost World?* Dinosaurs?"

"Nooo," I said snidely. "I'm not talking about dino-swahs."

"Well, what, then?"

"Spiritualism, old boy," I replied. "Contact with the dead."

"No way."

"Oh, way, alright. Doyle was a member of the Society for Psychical Research."

"How do you know this stuff?" asked the shrink.

Ignoring his question, I continued, "They say that Doyle was interested in the spirit world for a long time, but after his wife died, he really got into it. Didn't you ever see those fake faerie photos?"

"Fake faerie photos?" ask the psychiatrist.

"You know," I said. "Back in the early 1900's it was easier to fool the public with touched-up photos. One of the most well-known of those photos is of a little girl in a garden, looking at these little faeries flying around."

"I have seen that," the doctor proclaimed. "I remember seeing that picture somewhere."

"One of the reasons that particular photograph is so popular is because Conan Doyle wrote an article about it in *The Strand* magazine. It was in the Christmas issue."

"Did Doyle expose it as fake?"

"No!" I said, exasperated. "That's what I'm trying to tell you. Doyle believed it was real! Just like Shaver believed in the underground creatures he called the Dero."

"But Shaver spent time in a mental institution," said the shrink.

"If Conan Doyle had not already been famous for writing the Sherlock Holmes stories," I said, "they might have put him in a mental institution. Even as it was, a lot of people laughed at him. But not everyone."

"So do you believe in ghosts?" asked the psychiatrist. "Or that evil mutants live underground?"

"I've heard them."

Chapter Nine

1960s

The Hidden Phone

When Paul Clemens went missing, Roger, Eric, and I carried on his important work in gadgetry. Eric Littleton's record player had no output jacks. The speaker was built into the turntable base. The three of us removed the back of his record player and soldered long wires inside. We ran the wires to speakers out on the patio in Eric's back yard. We spliced in Christmas tree lights and hung them on a clothesline. The lights flashed to the rhythm of the music because of a rheostat Eric had.

I wanted to do something with wiring at my house.

My parents had purchased our house from Dr. Grayson because Grayson was moving higher on the hill. The doctor had a second telephone line installed for emergency calls from the hospital. It had a different phone number from ours. The doctor took his antique style rotary phone with him up the hill, and the hospital supposedly closed the account.

The old phone connection is in a wood-colored plastic junction box, the size of a deck of cards, attached to the baseboard behind a credenza in the living room. Above the credenza, a big picture window looks out over Danger Hill and the surrounding neighborhood of houses, lawns, roads, and sky.

Roger's dad, Sheriff in Charge of the City Jail, had an old phone the city gave him when they upgraded. He gave the phone to Roger, who walked into my house holding it behind his back.

"Guess what I got," and without waiting for an answer, presented the old phone resting on his upturned outstretched palm.

My parents had taken Jeff, Dennis, and Bruce to the county fair. They'd be gone for a while. Roger and I lifted the credenza away from the wall. We sat on the floor and unscrewed the cover of the junction box. Rolled up inside was a telephone line with one end disappearing into a hole in the wall. The phone number was written on a piece of tape. We connected the phone and got a dial tone. Even sitting down, Roger could see out the picture window, and the flower tops outside gave him an idea.

"Let's run the phone line underground into the flower bed and reconnect the phone out there."

"My dad has a drill bit for concrete."

Outside the house, below the picture window, is a brick flower bed. Early in the season, my mom always planted flowers that bloomed into a lush wave of vibrant colors. I dug a hole in the earth behind the flowers, close to the wall, down to where we had drilled a hole from inside, so Roger could feed the telephone wire through from the living room. I put the phone in a Johnny Quest lunchbox to keep dirt off, with a notch cut for the cord.

The lunchbox fit into the hole. I covered it with a piece of plywood and sprinkled dirt on top of it.

It was a fun novelty. Make and receive calls outside with only the few people who had the secret number. I put the lunchbox inside a plastic bag to keep out rainwater.

My parents slept with their door closed at the end of the hall. When I heard them snoring, I quietly opened the metal grate and dropped down into the basement. I reclosed the grate so my parents wouldn't fall in if they got up for any reason. That would have been horrible. From the basement I went into the backyard and circled around, uphill to the flower bed below the picture window. I called Nancy Griffin, and sometimes she called me at a planned time, because she had the number to the hidden phone.

She shared personal feelings with me on the phone. Her parents couldn't hear her, up in her heavily insulated attic Princess bedroom. She told me that she wanted to go to college and major in biology, but her father feared that some professor would make her choose Darwin over the Book of Genesis. Nancy, always levelheaded, shrugged off any suggestion that she couldn't believe in both evolution and creation. "Why can't they both be true?" She asked me. "I mean, it's been established that animals change over time. What difference if we call it evolution or God's studio?" Another time she said "God lives in every galaxy, and our brains are like galaxies, vastly filled with neon dots called synapses. So God can live in your brain, but also not in your brain."

I told her things like, "Three films are based on Mary Roberts Rinehart's play, *The Bat*, a mystery involving secret rooms in a dark mansion and a masked criminal. *The Bat*

(1926), a silent film, produced and directed by Roland West; *The Bat Whispers* (1930), this time with sound, again directed by West but produced by Joseph M. Schenk; and *The Bat* (1959) Starring Vincent Price and Agnes Moorehead, with a jazzed-up theme song by Alvino Rey, directed by Crane Wilber, produced by C.J. Tevlin…"

How Nancy endured this, I'll never know.

I never went to the Friday night high school football games because I didn't want to miss *The Outer Limits*, *The Twilight Zone*, and *Alfred Hitchcock Presents*. We didn't have streaming back then, so if you missed an episode, you couldn't see it for months. I knew Nancy went to the games with other guys and she even mentioned it once or twice. Life went on, but not really, not for me.

Chapter Ten

Four Cornered World

When I graduated from high school, my diary contained a four-leaf clover, pressed in wax paper between the pages, and one of those four-picture strips from a photo booth. The first two pictures are Nancy and me. Then Anne and Roger jumped in. The last two pictures show all four of us laughing and falling into each other.

Three years later, in Rota, Spain, Jim the Corpsman, Buddy Beckler, and I moved into a multistory apartment building in Rota, Spain. The buildings were radiant white in the sunshine. We were on the roof with some girls, rubbing suntan lotion on them and they on us, and we had big Bose Stereo speakers up there, cranked up loud. We were listening to Live Cream and Live Cream Volume II, and people on the roofs of other apartment buildings were waving to us and dancing. We were drinking rum & coke. One of the Spanish girls had diet pills that were legal to buy over the counter, amphetamines, and someone had hashish from Morocco. When Cream played *Tales of Brave Ulysses*, I remembered a line from Alfred Lord Tennyson's "Ulysses" about striving with gods, balanced by Percy Shelley's warning in "Ozymandias" that all great things must fall, so I knew we weren't gods but we were certainly sons of God, and it was awesome.

Another time, we were camping out on a beach in Algeciras, Spain under the black star-cluttered fabric of night. Jim, Buddy, and I had a campfire burning. We looked in awe across the fabulous eternal ocean, where the dark silhouette of the Rock of Gibraltar sat covered with its own stars, which were really lights from windows of houses, hotels, nightlife, and maybe campfires like ours.

A song by WAR called Four Cornered Room zoomed and whooshed and wailed from our battery-powered cassette tape player, blending with the wind and circling our heads with profound transcendence. Jim lit his pipe and passed it to me. My scalp tingled as the ocean-as-biggest-thing-in-the-world swelled around us and confirmed the outside, inside connection of our swimming DNA.

Chapter Eleven

Screaming Skulls

Living back home with my parents, I slowly realized I might never have to get a job. Medically discharged from the Navy, I received a small pension check every month. I signed the check over to my parents and lived in the same bedroom I grew up in. I had to visit a V.A. psychiatrist, Dr. Carnes, once a month for dissociative disorder.

Nancy was miles away, going to Hampton University on the east coast of Virginia near the Chesapeake Bay.

Roger and Anne were married with a four-year-old son, Tyler.

My brother Jeff had his own circle of friends.

Dad supervised a machine shop and Mom worked two days a week at a department store.

I mostly stayed home, listening to music through headphones, writing, and reading books about the supernatural. My routine included alcohol and weed.

The wall near my bed was full of bookshelves, with enough floorspace to stand between the bed and the shelves. Across the room near the door sat my roll-top desk, my chair, and a movie poster on the back of the door for *The Bat* (1959). I got out of bed on the side with bookshelves and reached up, placed two fingers on top of a thick hardback, Isaac Asimov's *The Foundation Trilogy*, and slid the book away from the others. Opening the book, I smiled at the silver flask of vodka nestled inside a cut-out section of pages. When I removed the flask, a joint rolled out.

"What will it be today?" I asked myself.

Screaming Skulls of Europe and Asia by Adam Sandhurst I decided. Followed by *Screaming Skulls of the New World* by Olsen Archer. Both books are historical records of skulls that fight against eviction from the walls and halls where they felt at home in life. From trash bins and burial pits, these skulls will shriek, knock over kitchen chairs by long distance, and spread decay over garden crops. When the skulls are brought back inside and placed in a cabinet, they keep quiet and the crops flourish.

All the legends in the Sandhurst book are rooted in Great Britain and historical Mesopotamia. English screaming skulls usually reside in manors and castles. In the newer book, Olsen Archer posits that because America is a relatively new country, it took longer for screaming skull stories to surface. But surface they did.

I am paraphrasing both authors from memory. That is why they don't sound like the world-class writers that they are.

The Screaming Skull of Burton Agnes Hall

In Yorkshire, England in 1599, Sir Henry Griffin builds a splendid mansion. The village of Burton Agnes is overrun with carpenters and stone masons. Builders watch Sir Griffin's three daughters when they walk from the smaller mansion, which he also owns. His wife lies in the nearby churchyard. He promises each of his three daughters a new bedroom in the new manor, to be called Burton Agnes Hall.

One of Sir Griffin's three daughters, Anne, goes for a walk. She is attacked and found in the park, dying from a serious knife wound. She is brought home to the small mansion.

Perhaps delirious with fever, Anne asks her sisters, when their father is not listening, "Pray thee sisters, should death and his men cart me into darkness, return at least my eyes into my sunlit bedroom of our new house, so shall I see the finished interior." Her sisters agree. At least her eyes. A short time later, Anne dies.

The two remaining sisters are holding a séance in the den, lit by a single candle, while Sir Griffin snores upstairs. More specifically, they are having a scrying session.

A bowl, made of dark blue stained glass, sits full to the brim of spring water, on the white tablecloth between the two girls. One sister holds a wand made from the branch of a laurel tree. She dips the resin-coated tip of the wand into the water and rubs it slowly around the rim of the bowl. Musical tones tinkle from the darkness around the girls.

"Now who will marry first?" asks the other sister.

Ripples form on the surface of the water and both girls lean in close.

The sisters later tell their father they heard bloodcurdling moans from the vicinity of Anne's tomb. The sounds did not stop until they exhumed Anne's body. To their shock and bafflement, the head had separated itself from the body and lost its skin.

"For the love of God, daughters! Why gone, her skin and tongue be, yet the eyeballs remain?"

"Daddy, 'tis surely the elements! You know how the fecund soil and conqueror worm doth ravage!"

"Enough, daughters, enough! I'll hear no more of it! For the love of God…" his voice fades down the hall.

Years passed at Burton Agnes Hall. Whenever someone tried to throw the skull away, the horses in the barn acted a fool and framed pictures in the dining room banged like a Jacob's Ladder click-clack toy.

They hid the skull behind bricks in one of the walls. The present-day owners of Burton Agnes Hall will not allow random stranger tourists to swagger through their home tapping walls.

I was hungry so I went to the kitchen. My mother always left two pieces of buttered toast and three strips of bacon, neatly arranged on a folded paper towel, on the Formica countertop by the sink.

I stared at the squiggly pattern in the old Formica countertop, looking for the face. I had played this game ever since I was a child. In the muted red, green, and black squiggles, there happened to be what looked like a little cartoon profile of a face, about the size of a dime. It had a black dot for an eye, a long flute-like nose, and a mouth opened in surprise or fear.

Sometimes I couldn't find the face in the Formica. At those times I would wonder if I remembered correctly. I would think *Is that it? No, is that it?* And finally - Aha! The real face leapt into focus, so familiar and true that it was like a missing puzzle piece, something you had almost written off as a faulty memory until you found it again.

"Are you ok?" my mother asked.

"My sinuses are 'acting up' a little because of my hay fever," I said. "Thanks for the bacon and toast."

I went back upstairs and cracked open the Olsen Archer volume, *Screaming Skulls of the New World*, and read Archer's account of

The Screaming Skull of Ames' Esso & Garage

Harold Ames, after a brief stint in the war, opened an Esso Gas Station and Garage on a highway near Irwin, Pennsylvania in 1944. An Exxon station still operates near there, but in 1944, they called it Esso. Harold Ames fixed automobiles, everything from changing spark plugs to rebuilding engines. His daughter Laura-Lee Ames waited on customers at the gas pumps.

In 1946, Willis Gimble switched uniforms, from Army to Esso. He went to work for Harold Ames, pumping gas, and married Ames' daughter, Laura-Lee. All three lived in Harold Ames' house on a side-road that split off from the highway and ran behind the house and garage and further into the woods. There were no other houses on the road, and it was closed to the public. There was only one vehicle among them. Laura-Lee drove the 1937 Ford to work at a diner. Harold Ames' wife bought the car before she died.

In the garage, Harold poured himself a glass of whiskey and sneered at the military surplus Harley-Davidson motorcycle that Willis brought in. Willis was thinking about buying the motorcycle, so he borrowed it and asked Harold to look it over from a mechanic's view. This Harley-Davidson was made for the U.S. Army during World War II. It was a standard WLA Harley with a 45 cubic inch V-twin engine.

Harold Ames was not happy. Willis Gimble wanted to go to Penn State University because the G.I. Bill would pay for it. That was a long way to travel. Harold thought it was only a matter of time before Laura-Lee and Willis rode away on that Harley, and Harold would be alone in the world.

"What about it?" said Willis.

"It still needs some work on the throttle," said Harold. "I'd feel safer if you left it here in the garage until I work it out."

Later, in their room with no Harold around, Willis told Laura-Lee, "There ain't a damn thing wrong with that throttle. The old bastard don't want to let go of the bike."

One night, Harold parked his car behind the garage and drank himself into stupor. Snoring face down on the workbench when a noise woke him up. He heard someone roll the Harley outside and kickstart it. The engine rumbled as he passed out again. When he woke up early the next morning, the motorcycle was back in the garage.

"So, your hubby took a little test drive last night," said Harold the next day.

"What are you talking about?" asked Laura-Lee, looking puzzled.

Another night Harold looked in Harley's leather saddlebags and found a brand-new roadmap. Someone had opened the map and refolded it the wrong way, but it was clearly new. Harold ransacked the contents of the glove box in the '37 Ford. What were these little flaps of slick cardboard? They were wallpaper samples.

Soon, Laura-Lee was hanging wallpaper in the bedroom she shared with her husband Willis.

Harold Ames was delighted. He offered to buy all the wallpaper they needed and help her do other rooms in the house. She happily agreed. His daughter obviously wasn't planning to leave this place anytime soon. After several days of shopping, bringing home wallpaper samples, and more shopping, Laura-Lee had picked out a different color scheme for every room. But then she started saying she didn't feel good or was too tired to hang wallpaper. She argued with Willis.

When Laura-Lee got a busted lip, she swore it was from bumping it on a rafter in the attic looking for picture hangers.

When her chin got bruised, she didn't know how she got it. Harold didn't believe her.

Harold and Willis put up the *closed for business* sign around sundown when Laura-Lee showed up in the '37 Ford. They set a cow skull near the road to frighten tourists low on gas.

"Heh, heh, heh, move along," the cow skull grins, "no gasoline no water…death walks tonight…"

One night they came home, and Harold got drunk and stupid.

"If you ever hurt my daughter!"

"Daddy, stop it now. Willis would never hurt…"

"Did he hit you baby?"

"Come on, old man, I love Laura-Lee…"

"Aaaah, get off me! Go to Penn State, motherfucker, before I kill you!"

"If that's the way you feel, maybe I should move out!" said Willis.

Laura-Lee was in tears, "No, baby, don't go. Stay here. Tell him daddy. Everybody just go to bed!"

Apparently, everyone went to bed.

Around 2:00 AM, Harold Ames woke up. He crept out to the garage carrying a whiskey bottle.

The rumbling offbeat rhythm of the Harley's V-twin engine thundered through a dark, moonless night. No streetlights, just a single headlight on the old side road from Harold Ames' garage toward the highway.

Closer to the highway, hidden among trees and shrubs, Harold drank from his whiskey bottle and heard the motorcycle getting closer. He saw the headlight coming.

"Nobody runs off and leaves my daughter," he mumbled.

The rider's headlight scanned a thin copper wire, stretched across the road between two trees.

The Harley-Davidson kept going at first, as the rider's head spun once and hit the road. Maybe the headless rider's hand went slack on the throttle. The motorcycle slowed, leaned to the right, and lay in the grass.

Harold Ames ran from his hiding place and knelt to get a closer look at the head of that bastard,

Willis. But what he saw instead was the wide-eyed head of his daughter, Laura-Lee!

It wasn't Willis Gimble who tried to leave. It was Laura-Lee, going to join her lover, a wallpaper salesman in the city of Irwin. She still had wallpaper samples in the saddlebag.

Harold Ames was arrested later that day. He died in jail awaiting trial. One story said he had bite marks.

Willis Gimble inherited the house and garage but lost the gas station to an oil conglomerate. He attempted to burn the entire place down and almost succeeded.

Mysteriously, one room didn't burn. The Screaming Skull of Ames' Esso and Garage rests in a hinged box made of wood from the walls of that room. The box is lined inside with scorched wallpaper.

Chapter Twelve

The Olsen Archer Connection

Roger heard about the opening of the Olson Archer Museum from Meg Longino, who heard it on Talk Radio OK6AM. He insisted we go to Hampton and meet the man himself. Nancy was still a student at Hampton University, living on campus, and she supposedly knew someone who knew Olson Archer. We called Nancy long distance. She said, "bring sleeping bags, I can sneak you into my dorm room, to save money on a hotel." She said it was about a five-hour drive. Spring break was coming up. There was going to be a party on campus that we all could attend.

"You can interview Archer," said Roger. "We can bring back the *Astral Beat.*"

"What if he doesn't do interviews?"

"Don't call it an interview. When you meet him, ask for his autograph, and just ask him some questions. I'll write down his answers. Maybe even record it."

"That's not a bad idea."

Roger took some vacation days from his job. Anne stayed home with their son Tyler. We took the metallic-green 1968 Chevy Bel Air that Anne's parents had given her.

We drove Eastward across the state of Virginia. Every time a radio station began to fade, it was my job to tune in another one. A green sign overhead said *Hampton/Hampton University/Next 2 Exits*. Per instructions we took the first exit and followed the signs.

Per instructions we were close to Nancy's dorm.

A man and woman stood on the sidewalk in front of the building. It was Nancy and a young black man doing a one-armed hug. He had a briefcase in his other hand, she was holding a backpack strap with her free hand, to keep it from slipping off her shoulder.

"See you later tonight," she said to him.

They looked at me strangely because I got there so fast out of the car to hear their conversation.

"Okay, Nance," he said.

The young man wore a heavy blend Crewneck, beige with double helix designs. I thought it looked better than my cotton Polo shirt with blue and white triangles, and it annoyed me to get one-upped by sweater.

"Oh," said Nancy. "Here are my friends Whit and Roger. Let me introduce you."

His name was Craig. An anthropology major.

"I'm happy to meet you, Whit and Roger," he said. "Wow, you're tall. I hope to see you at the party tonight at the clubhouse."

"Cool!" said Roger.

"Got to go," he said. "Later."

He walked away briskly.

"Well, that was a surprise," I said.

"What?" said Nancy.

"Him, that guy, it's kind of surreal."

"Hampton University," said Nancy "is historically African American."

"What? No, that's not what I meant. I'm saying it looks like you have a boyfriend."

"I guess I forgot to mention it," said Roger.

"Just a friend," said Nancy. "Craig's a great guy. Come on."

I knew I had no right to be jealous. Nancy couldn't wait for me. I stayed in my parents' house reading about screaming skulls, watching The Twilight Zone, and drinking. Once we got to her room, Nancy made coffee and brought out some blueberry muffins. The three of us talked and caught up. I went to the bathroom and took a swig from my flask. I chased the vodka with tap water, cupped in my hands. It was good to see Nancy again.

"Roger," said Nancy, "tell Anne, good job on your hair. Whit, I can smell alcohol from here. The party is in the Church Annex building. Let's go."

We walked a few blocks to a long wood-framed building with a zig-zag roof, like the annex at Nancy's church. Inside, an older man introduced himself pleasantly as "Dr. Billum, Dean of Student Activities." Nancy saw Craig and waved to him from across the room. He smiled and walked toward us.

The gathering was mostly students and a few faculty members. There was a buffet, tables with tablecloths, a lounge area with easy chairs, and what may have been a dance floor. Conversation was not difficult over the music from the record player. It was a jazzy tune with an electric guitar spiraling nicely.

Nancy showed me a stack of record albums. They had Contemporary Gospel, Traditional Gospel, Christian Rock, Old Time Religion, Inspirational, Spiritual, Street, Jesus Freak, John Mayall's Jazz/Blues Fusion, and Stevie Wonder.

"Quite a selection, isn't it?" said Craig, walking up behind me.

"Yeah," I said, turning to him.

He turned to Nancy, both of them smiling at each other, and said, "We have almost forty people here tonight. I'm happy with that."

"Who is playing guitar in this record?" I asked.

"That's Phil Keaggy. Funny you should ask. Dad digs Phil Keaggy."

"Who?"

"My dad, Olsen Archer. He listens to this album in his hospital room."

"Hospital room?"

"Oh, you didn't know?"

"Did you say your dad?"

"Yeah, right right."

"In the hospital?"

"Well, I'm sorry to be the one to tell you, Whit. Dad's got pancreatic cancer. It's inoperable."

"Oh, no," I said. "That's terrible."

"Yeah, but his mind is still sharp, and he wants us to visit him."

"Really?"

"Yeah."

"I'm just sorry to hear about, about…"

"He told me to tell everyone to cheer up and rejoice in the Lord," said Craig.

"Wow."

"His house is going to be a museum. It's pretty exciting. The State of Virginia has declared his house a Literary Landmark and the opening ceremony is in three days."

"Will he be there?"

"If he's up to it, yeah. But we're going to visit him at the hospital, the day before the ceremony. I got it all set up."

"Outstanding!" I beamed. "I mean, I'm sorry. I didn't know."

"It's okay, Whit. I know you didn't. It's cool to meet a fan of my dad's work, though, so tell me about yourself. Nancy says you dig Poe?"

My flask was empty, and I could see there was no drinking going on at this party. But I didn't mind. Excited about meeting Olsen Archer, I drank several cups of coffee, ate two pieces of cake, and talked to Craig for a while.

We jettisoned the idea of sneaking back into Nancy's room that night. Dr. Billum said if Nancy, Roger, and I wanted to stay and help Craig clean up after the party, then Roger and I could bring our sleeping bags into the building and spend the night there, while Nancy and Craig would each return to their respective dorms. Roger slept on a long sectional couch, and I slept on a cot.

I enjoyed a deep and restful sleep, accompanied by some clear and colorful dreams, the details of which I still remember, sometimes, and don't think about other times.

We ate breakfast the next morning around 9:00 AM in the lounge area of Nancy's dormitory.

Chapter Thirteen

Olsen Archer

Sunlight filled the spacious lobby of the ultra-modern Careplex hospital, beaming in through tall rectangular windows separated by equal sized maple panels, creating an alternating pattern of windows and wood all around us.

Craig led Nancy, Roger, and me past the information desk, straight to the elevator. Under one arm I carried a cassette tape recorder, a yellow legal pad with a ballpoint pen clipped to it, and a copy of Olsen Archer's *Screaming Skulls of the New World.*

We arrived at Olsen Archer's room. The writer sat propped up in bed, watching television, sipping a cup of coffee. The ceramic cup looked small in his big hand, and he held it delicately with his thumb and two middle fingers. This was because a thin wire taped to his index finger was plugged into a monitor with lights and numbers. His other arm had an IV line in it.

Archer looked a lot like the picture on the back of his book, but now his hair was completely white and his once-square jaw was a little more padded. When he turned to look at us, he arched one eyebrow inquisitively, then broke into a warm smile.

"Come in, come in," said the author. "Hi, Craig. These must be the friends you told me about."

"Mr. Archer," I said. "I can't believe I'm meeting you. I've read your books."

"The pleasure is mine," he said. "Please, call me Olsen. I'm always happy to meet someone who reads my books. Do you have a favorite?"

"This one, I brought with me. I was hoping you would sign it."

"Ah, the *Screaming Skulls*, I'd be happy to sign it. What's the name of your periodical?"

"*The Astral Beat.*"

"Nice," said Archer. "The word astral covers everything from outer space phenomena like UFO's, to astrology, to the ethereal spirit that lives on after physical death."

I was beside myself that Olsen Archer had voiced the nuances of my newspaper's title.

"That's exactly it," I said. "Thank you."

Roger said, "Whit would be thrilled if he could interview you."

"That would be great," said Olsen, and looking over my head at Roger, "Wow are you tall. Did you play basketball in high school?"

"I did," said Roger. "Tried to, anyway."

Archer buzzed for a nurse and asked her if we could borrow a couple of extra chairs so everyone could sit down.

"I see you have a tape recorder," he said. "Why don't you set it here."

I set the tape recorder on a rolling food try.

"Roll it closer to me," he said.

I rolled the narrow table close to his bedside.

"I guess I push play and record at the same time, eh?" he said, clicking the buttons down with his left hand.

"You met Richard Shaver, didn't you?" I asked.

"Yes, I did," said Archer. "In 1970, long after he wrote for *Amazing Stories*. He was about sixty years old, but I used to joke around by calling him a 'hardened beatnik.' Not that he was ever a beatnik, but he had that white Vandyke beard and mustache, a full head of hair combed back like a 1950's hotrod mechanic, and that stern, long face. I say hardened, because at various times, Shaver had been a welder, a hobo, factory worker, and a psychiatric patient, before he turned to writing and art; so, you know, he was a Renaissance man. He lived in a little ramshackle house with a tin roof, in Summit, Arkansas."

"The Rock House Studio," I said.

"Yeah, I've heard it called that," said Archer. "He showed me a rock, about the size of a grapefruit. It looked to me like it may have come from a riverbed because it was smooth and rounded. Shaver had cracked it down the middle into two parts. He called it a rock book. He had lots of them. He cracked them open, looked inside, and saw images in the patterns of the exposed rock. He said the images were encoded into the rocks, centuries ago, by extraterrestrials. These aliens were stranded on Earth when their ship left without them. They lived in underground caverns to avoid the sun and devolved into mutants called Dero, which enjoyed torturing humans both physically and mentally, and were given to kinky sexual proclivities."

"O... kay . . ." said Nancy, rolling her eyes.

"I know, right?" said Olsen with a laugh. "But art is art, and some of Shaver's pieces are quite surreal, quite interesting. Full of phantasmagorical demons and nudes and parts of human faces, all intertwined. They had a spackled texture. He showed me one of his finished pieces. As I studied the earthy, pastel colors, I suddenly saw a rainbow in the rock. He had coated the surface with a layer of detergent. He experimented with ink, dye, wax, and detergent. And that brings us to one of the chapters in my latest book, Whit. I hope you will include this in the *Astral Beat*. In one chapter I discuss similarities between the Shaver Mystery and the disappearance of school children in . . ."

Archer leaned back and looked at the ceiling.

"Oh, gee," he said, closing his eyes for a moment. "I don't think I'm supposed to say anything about it yet."

"Why not?" asked Roger.

"Well, it might be in my contract. But you know what? Nothing is stopping you from going into my office late tonight, when no one is there, and looking in the access panel behind my desk."

"Are you serious?" asked Roger.

I was speechless.

Craig said, "We should stick to the contract, though, which I assume is with the Literary Society as a corporation?"

"What are they going to do to me?" Archer laughed. "I'll be famous longer than they will. Just don't tell anyone we spoke of this until… some time passes."

"I give you my word," I said almost crying.

"But what exactly are we doing?" asked Craig.

"Craig and Nancy, you should return to your respective dorms. Both of you have academic considerations regarding the appearance of impropriety. I would ask that Whit and Roger carry out this intrigue, just the two of them. No offense to you guys, Whit and Roger."

Nobody said anything.

"Now, listen close," continued Olsen, "and by the way, I'm enjoying this very much, thank you. They put new locks on all the doors to my house. The real estate agent hasn't brought me a key so you will need to use the secret entrance."

"No way," said Craig.

"Oh, yes, way. A secret passageway. If you go into my back yard, you'll see a two-tiered water fountain with a gargoyle on top. The fountain stands in the middle of a round concrete pool in the ground. The pool is only a foot deep and three feet across, but there's no water in it, anyway. Been dry for years. If you stand on the edge of the pool, grab the fountain's top tier," Olsen leaned forward with outstretched hands, holding the invisible curve of stone leaves, "and then lean back, see? Pull it back. As you lean backward, the concrete base opens over a round hole in the ground. There's a tunnel down there that leads to the house."

"Nice," said Roger.

"Yeah," said Archer. "Craig helped me do it. I've only shared it with a few of my colleagues, not too many. Now, I need some sleep."

He leaned back on his pillow and closed his eyes, and said, "In the back yard, exit through the shed. Happy hunting."

As we filed out of Archer's hospital room, I almost collided with a full-figured woman wearing a smartly tailored blue business skirt and jacket, and a name tag. I thought nothing of it at the time.

Chapter Fourteen

Secret Passage

Just after midnight, Roger and I parked the metallic-green Chevy Bel Air in front of a closed Starbucks. Olsen Archer's house was at the edge of an old neighborhood, adjacent to a city revitalization project. In a field where kids once played stickball, tourists would now stroll past shops, restaurants, and the Olsen Archer House Museum. Tonight, nothing stirred except us under misty mercury vapor streetlights.

A shrouded specter stood in the dark front lawn of Olsen's house. We froze in our tracks.

"What the hell is that?" I whispered.

Roger stepped up to the cloaked figure.

"It's just a tarp," he said.

"Covering what?"

He lifted a section of the tarp, revealing a cast metal "historical literary landmark" sign, mounted on a pole.

"I guess they'll unveil it tomorrow."

Roger let the tarp fall back over the sign and we proceeded around the house to the back yard.

"What's that noise?" whispered Roger.

"It sounds like running water," I said. "Hey, look at that! I thought he said the fountain was dry."

Water flowed out of the gargoyle's mouth like a small waterfall and filled the top tier, which overflowed into the lower tier, then into the pool on the ground.

"They must have fixed it for the grand opening," said Roger. "Olsen didn't know."

"Oh, man," I whispered, agitated. "Are those goldfish in there?"

"No, I don't think so," said Roger. "Just leaves."

"Can we still do this, I mean without breaking a pipe or something?"

"I think so. We might get wet from the spillage, but we've come this far…"

Roger stood on the edge of the ground pool, gripped the top tier, and leaned back. I pushed from the other side. Earth crumbled under my feet as the fountain toppled toward Roger. I slid uncontrollably down into a dark earthy hole. Tree roots broke my fall as I broke through the roots and landed hard, sitting down. Water poured onto my head from a broken PVC pipe. I looked up, moving my face out from under the running water.

"I was hoping it was a hose and not a pipe," said Roger from what seemed far above me. "Are you okay? Hold on, I'll unholster my flashlight."

Two big goldfish suddenly stirred up mud in the shallow water beside me.

"Oh God!"

The fish scared me.

I stood up fast and climbed faster, hands and feet finding roots, rocks, holes in the wall, until I crawled out onto the grass. I rolled over on my back, breathing hard.

"Those were fish!" I said.

"That shit must be at least six feet deep. Did you see a door?"

"Piece of wood, but we've got to save the fish."

Roger's darting flashlight caught a shed on the far corner of the back yard. On the ground beside the shed, a bell pepper garden, staked in rows. A galvanized metal watering pitcher posed beside a new wheelbarrow for public viewing. We filled the pitcher with water from the PVC pipe and filled the wheelbarrow. I picked up the fish one at a time with a bowhead class hand trowel and transferred them to the wheelbarrow.

"Maybe when we get inside," I said, "we can make an anonymous call for the fish, they might need aeration."

Roger gave me his flashlight. I lowered myself back into the hole and pulled a long board away from an opening in the wall. After bending down and stepping through the opening, I could stand up. Wooden planks lined the walls and ceiling of the tunnel going forward, like a mineshaft. Roger came in behind me and complained bitterly about having to crouch-walk. I rarely ever heard him complain.

The tunnel ended with stone steps leading to a door above my head. The door easily opened when I pushed up, and my upper body emerged inside a cabinet under the sink in a room for plants and aquariums.

Olsen's book bio said he dabbled in horticulture and aquascape. The Literary Society had spruced up his Conservatory, as he called it, based on the *Clue* board game. The mechanical greenhouse roof was closed. Olsen had a great poster on the wall, framed. It was a blown-up section of the 1949 vintage Clue board game: Conservatory.

We crawled out of the cabinet. Roger stood up straight and I heard his spine crack. Our faces and bodies reflected soft aquarium light from multiple tanks. Shadows of fish rippled over us in slow glides.

I opened another door and saw Olsen Archer's study for the first time. But someone else opened a door to the study from somewhere in the dark. I backed up into the conservatory and shut the door. We saw a light come on under the door and could hear someone stirring around.

A tense minute passed. We whispered that maybe this new intruder would leave quickly. After another minute, we whispered that if we get in legal trouble for this, we will not incriminate Olsen. And even if we say nothing, we speculated, the district attorney may discern that Olsen was behind it. But if no one discerns it, Olson himself would probably break the silence and take the blame. But if he didn't, and we can't lie under oath, Olsen Archer will be the brightest star in the *Astral Beat* galaxy of psychics. No, Forteans. We had a whisper argument in the dark about which designation was better: psychic vs. Fortean. I think one of us said *Psychorteans*.

A crashing noise came from the other room. It was, we later learned, Glenda Wells, knocking over a chair and running out the front door. We ventured into the study. Roger saw the thick packet on the floor. I felt around inside the wall panel to make sure we got it all.

The front door was open and there were cars and people in the street.

"Back that way," said Roger.

In the conservatory we found a new aquarium, still in the box.

"Twenty-Gallon Tank," the box said.

Carrying the empty tank in tandem, we hurried back into the tunnel, Roger cursing the low ceiling. To climb out of the hole, Roger took hold of a root above his head, and with the aquarium hanging in his other hand, hoisted himself out. I crawled out behind him. We filled the tank with clean water for the goldfish.

We remembered Olsen saying, "leave through the shed." In the back of the shed we found an exit door, which opened onto a completely different street, with vines and flowerpots hanging over the door. You wouldn't even think it went to Olsen's back yard shed. A door-spring pulls it shut and locked, no door handle on the outside. We strolled down an avenue of trees, closed shops, an open bar, around the corner to our car.

Chapter Fifteen

The Plague on the Stairs

The next morning Nancy and Craig went early to the hospital. Roger and I got there an hour later. Craig held the door open for us and reclosed it behind us. Inside, Olsen was happy and buoyant, sitting up in bed, music playing on the radio.

"My, my," he chuckled. "We were just listening to the radio news about some skullduggery that occurred last night at the Archer house."

"Did we delay the grand opening?" asked Roger.

"Not by much," said Craig.

"It's good publicity," said Olsen. "Just one more mystery associated with My House."

Nancy added, "They said on the radio Ms. Wells is stable, so that's good."

"Did you guys do anything to frighten her?" asked Craig.

"No," said Roger. "We don't know why she screamed."

"It scared us."

"We have a theory," said Olsen. "We talked about it before you guys got here. Show them the picture in the paper, Nancy."

The newspaper article about the Olsen house disturbance included a photograph of Olsen's study, taken earlier that morning. Specifically, it was a picture of his desk, taken at such an angle as to show the open access panel behind the desk.

"Do you see those two framed pictures leaning against the wall on the floor? Look at the one closest to the access panel."

It was a wavy pattern of intricate shapes and colors.

"It's a new kind of art," said Archer. "Almost like magic. You put your face close to it, then back off slowly, trying not to focus your eyes directly on the lines and shapes. If you do it right, a seemingly 3-D image will appear in the design!"

"It's new," said Craig. "Those are original prints."

"Yes," said Olsen. "I think that unfortunate woman saw it, quite by accident, when she knelt in front of the access panel. She was already jumpy and scared, trying to steal the magazine as a steppingstone to fame, which I would have accommodated had she asked."

"And the image in that picture," said Craig, "is a 3-D likeness of a 19th Century book illustration called *The Plague on the Stairs* by Theodor Kittelsen. It depicts the bubonic plague as a death's head specter in a shroud, creeping up the stairs to infect another household."

"The face is horrible," said Nancy.

"But you got the magazine, right?"

Roger reached inside his white buckskin vest and brought out the tightly wrapped manilla envelope with a folded magazine inside.

Chapter Sixteen

The Malta Connection

The envelope we found in Olsen Archer's house contained a vintage August 1940 issue of *National Geographic* magazine, folded longways. It had an article about the island of Malta, with a brief mention about school children getting lost in the ancient underground burial caverns, known as the Hypogeum, with additional notes handwritten in the margins by Olsen himself.

"May I see it?" asked Craig.

Roger had removed the magazine from the envelope. He handed it to Craig.

"That issue of *National Geographic* is not particularly rare," Olsen told us. "By itself, that magazine boasts nothing to earmark it as a collector's item. But to my knowledge, the notes I wrote in the margins are the first time anyone has referenced the Shaver Mystery in connection to Malta. And that makes it valuable as an artifact. I was supposed to present it to Literary Society during the ceremony today, but I decided you four should have it. Nobody knew where I hid it, so Ms. Wells must have been outside the door when I told you. She wants to be on the paranormal radar. I think she's writing a book."

Craig sat in an upholstered chair with leg crossed over knee, magazine open, reading. Roger rested comfortably in the other upholstered chair with his head laid back on the top of the backrest. Nancy sat on the edge of Olsen's bed, both hands around a cup of hot chocolate. I chose a vinyl cushioned Bertoia side chair.

"This is interesting," said Craig. "In 1935, a schoolteacher took a group of kids on a field trip into the Hypogeum. They apparently got lost down there and were never seen again. After that, the government closed certain tunnels to the public. People still claim to hear the cries of children."

"Samuel Taylor Coleridge went to Malta," I said.

Roger just listened and didn't say anything.

Nancy said, "Craig, you said earlier you would tell us about the Hypogeum?"

"Well," said Craig, "I mean, if these guys feel like it."

"Go ahead," said Roger.

"Thanks, Roger," said Craig. "Well, the Hypogeum was discovered by accident in 1902 on the island of Malta. A construction worker was digging a foundation for a house and broke through into a chamber containing thousands of skeletons. Some of the bones date back to 3000 BC, the Megalithic Age. Besides the tombs, there's a vast network of underground chambers and passageways, carved in rock, three levels deep. Some of the walls are painted with swirling lines and web-like patterns, all in shades of yellow-gold and reddish-orange ochre, one of the earliest pigments."

Nancy beamed with admiration at Craig's display of knowledge. This made me a little jealous. Roger didn't help much when he said, "Damn, Craig, you know your shit, man!"

"I want to know more about the people disappearing underground," I said. "That's what we should focus on, right?"

I flipped open a small notebook from my shirt pocket and wrote something on a blank page.

Nancy walked over to a chair where her handbag sat.

"Look what I've got."

She pulled out some travel brochures for the Maltese Islands and passed them around. I opened a glossy trifold and saw pictures of sunny beaches, beautiful blue water, sailboats and yachts, forts, castles, and captivating architecture in shades of cream, tan, brown, and brick-red.

"At this time," Olsen rejoined the conversation, "the public can tour a small, safe part of the Hypogeum. There may be someone we can contact about getting a better view. There is a list of government agencies on the back of that brochure."

Roger sat up in his chair and read out loud from the brochure, "Ministry for Urban Development."

"Yeah, I saw that too," I said.

"Craig," said Roger. "You said the Hypogeum was accidentally discovered on a housing site?"

"Yeah."

"And it shows the location of Urban Development Ministry as House of the Four Winds; Valletta, Malta."

"It's the number four again," said Roger.

"Not just that," I said. "Paul Clemens carved Four Winds into the dome wall."

"I'd almost forgotten about that," said Nancy. It made me feel alone.

Craig stood up and walked over to the side of the bed where Olsen had adjusted to a more prone position. He asked his dad, "Couldn't you have just told them about Malta and the *National Geographic* article?"

"Yeah," said Olsen, "but it was more fun this way."

Chapter Seventeen

Preflight

Roger drove Nancy and me back to Hansburg. Nancy wanted to visit her parents. Spring break would last ten days. Craig stayed in Hampton. His dad bought him a ticket to Malta and was setting up some church-related college field trip. I didn't understand it, but my parents were willing to buy me a plane ticket to Malta and give me money, just to get me out of their house for a while. Nancy's father, the church pastor, and her mother, the church secretary, were doing quite well financially. The church was prospering because this was around 1985. After the bacchanalia of the '70s, people looked for direction and joined churches in record numbers. The island of Malta is where Paul the Apostle was shipwrecked in the Book of Acts in the Bible. On that basis, Nancy's parents agreed to pay for a church-related Malta pilgrimage. They warned her to stay away from pagan temples and pagans.

Roger showed up at my door, beaming.

"You won't believe what happened," he said. "My yearly two-week Army Reserve duty is coming due, so I called up my Captain, said please get me a flight. He got me a seat on a MAC flight to Sigonella, Sicily, the Navy base. All I have to do is attend a three-day NATO Data Processing class in Sigonella. Then I'm free for the rest of the tour. I can get to Malta from Sigonella in five hours. I take a train and then a ferry."

"Why is this Captain being so nice?"
"He wants me to reenlist, full-time in the Army. He said if he takes care of me now, I owe him when the next patriot drive comes along."

"Are you going to re-enlist?" I asked.
"No."

Ironically, Roger had to go to Langley Air Force Base, near Hampton, Virginia, to catch the Military Airlift Command flight. We didn't miss a beat.

Chapter Eighteen

Malta

Our plane touched down in Malta at night. I woke up in my window seat as the plane taxied toward the air terminal, bright lights glaring off the window and obscure dark shapes moving on the tarmac. Roger would join us when his Army Reserve commitment was fulfilled.

Nancy, Craig, and I went to baggage claim. Craig and I both reached for Nancy's luggage at the same time and bumped into each other. A friendly and energetic cab driver plucked up two of our suitcases with impressive strength.

"Allow me," he beamed. "My name is Nicolo. My taxi is right outside. Do you have hotel reservations?"

"The Park Hotel in Valletta," said Nancy.

"Very good," he said. "Only three miles from here."

Nicolo radiated competence and confidence, with his proud shiny baldness and neatly trimmed black mustache, black suit-style uniform, and Italian leather shoes with tassels. In no time, he loaded our baggage into the trunk of his Renault cab and opened the front passenger door for Nancy.

Craig and I sat in the back seat, weary and jet-lagged, but Nancy had become animated, asking our taxi driver all kinds of questions as we drove to the hotel.

"We're interested in the Hypogeum," said Nancy.

"That is a very popular site," said the driver. "It's not far. I suggest you make reservations for the tour, first thing in the morning. They only allow so many visitors each day. Usually booked for ahead couple of days. But there are many other things to do in the meantime."

"Like what?"

"Are you college students?" asked Nicolo.

"Yes, we are," said Nancy, even though I was not, but she and Craig were.

"Then let me suggest this," said Nicolo. "All of Malta is a museum. Do not spend all your time indoors. The scenery, the customs, and the architecture of Malta are a rich mixture of different styles, influenced by our history of changing cultures and nationalities."

"What is the House of the Four Winds?" I asked.

"The House of the Four Winds? It is an office building now, for various departments of the government. At one time, it housed the Ministry of Justice. Years ago, it was a private residence."

"I see," said Nancy. "Not really a tourist attraction, then?"

"Not that I'm aware of," the driver said. "The only reason I know as much as I do about Four Winds is due to a young man named Clemens, who works at the taxi motor pool. He is very knowledgeable and enjoys sharing his knowledge."

"Did you say Clemens?" asked Nancy.

"Yes, Clemens is a young American fellow who maintains the taxicabs."

The next morning was like a sunny dream.

We stepped out of the hotel and walked under a clear blue sky among Baroque palaces; medieval castles; Renaissance cathedrals topped with majestic domes; villas, like I had seen in Spain, made of white stucco, with arched doorways, red tile roofs, and patios. As we turned down one narrow street, a group of children ran playing from the other direction. Their laughter echoed off the amber colored bricks of a tall building with iron window grills painted dark green. Compact cars and minibikes drove on the left side of the road amid statues, palm trees, fountains, and foreign street signs.

For a set price, the taxi driver Nicolo became our guide and transportation to several towns, all within a fifteen-mile radius. We walked around each town until we got tired and then rode in Nicolo's Renault to the next destination. We kept the same formation as the night before, Nancy in the front passenger seat, Craig and I in the back seat.

"I looked for Mr. Clemens at the motor pool," said Nicolo, glancing in the rear-view mirror as he drove. "To ask what city he is from in America. But he didn't come to work today."

We looked at each other.

"We've got to find out," I said.

"Absolutely. Tomorrow, probably," said Nicolo as he veered smoothly into a parking space next to the curb. "For now, let us stroll down Republic Avenue."

Republic Avenue in Valletta could have almost been New York City with its banner flags and roll-up metal gates above the storefronts, until your eyes follow the second-story row of balconies under ornate cornices, to the life size statue of Queen Victoria that presided over the square from atop a raised pedestal. Behind the statue was the National Library of Malta. We mingled with the people in the square, in front of the statue of Queen Victoria, sampling snacks and coffee from vendors. I ate some small, diamond-shaped pastries filled with ricotta cheese, called pastizzi.

Nancy and Craig were obviously enjoying a carefree familiarity. I walked behind them. When Craig pointed out some fascinating sight, they looked at each other, faces almost touching.

Back in the car, we drove southwest alongside a sparkling strip of ocean known as the Grand Harbor. We looked out the windows on the left side of the car, across the water, at the breathtaking angular walls and turrets of Fort St. Angelo, in stony shades of white and light gray, tinged with faint traces of blue and tan, stacked like irregular blocks of a massive layer cake, topped with flags, surrounded by dockyards and sailboats.

We drove southeast to Paol and made reservations to tour the Hypogeum.

It was a whirlwind of a day.

As the sun went down, Nancy and Craig retired to their rooms.

"I want to hit the Four Winds Pub," I said. "Anyone care to join me?"

"Why don't we all go there tomorrow night?" said Nancy. "I'm beat. I need some sleep."

"Me, too," said Craig. "But knock yourself out."

"Here," said Nancy, reaching into her purse. "Take this coupon. It gets you a free beer."

"Thanks, Nance,"

I put the coupon in my shirt pocket, left the hotel and walked to the Four Winds Pub.

Inside the pub was dark enough for privacy and softly lit around the bar, walkways, and decor. The walls were inlaid mosaic tile, as was the backdrop for the liquor bottles behind the long, polished oak bar. Some tables had lanterns casting soft light. Oversized vases stood on either side of the main door and the kitchen door. I asked for a Farson's Ale because it is brewed there in Malta. It was strong and tasty, so I ordered another one and found a table.

A mixture of locals and vacationers filled the place. In one corner, a loud group of businesspeople in suits and skirts were unwinding and toasting one another. At another table, two men and two women, dressed in tuxedos and formal evening dresses, were talking to a server. Others milled around in Hawaiian shirts, Bermuda shorts, t-shirts, and jeans.

I relaxed at the table with my third beer, thinking I should be more friendly toward Craig. I knew I was wrong to resent his reportage. A lot of his information was interesting to me.

A "leprechaun" man startled me badly. I had noticed him earlier, sitting at another table with his back to me, smoking hashish. It smelled good but I didn't know the etiquette. He glanced back at me.

Without warning, the man closed the gap between himself and me like a predatory animal. I suddenly found his dark, leathery face a couple of inches from my own. He held something to my throat. It felt sharp. I knew it had to be a knife. He smiled and showed me the object in his hand. It was my own ink pen. He was even shorter than me but with a large chest and arms bulging in a dark green suit and a dark green derby hat with a buckle in front of the hatband.

"You dropped," he said, with a raspy, clipped accent, "on floor at bar." He smiled and said again, "You dropped" in a relaxing tone.

The pen must have fallen from my shirt pocket at the bar when I remembered the coupon Nancy gave me. This guy thought he was funny, scaring me shitless.

"I buy you beer," he growled. "I joker but people don't know, I know this."

We were both standing. He sat down at my table.

"Please," he said with hand outstretched to the other chair. "Waiter! Two Farsons!"

I'm thinking, well he returned my pen. And another beer. I sat down.

"Hypogeum?" he said.

"What?"

"You want to know about Dero living underground in the Richard Shaver chronicles."

"How do you know that? Who are you?"

"Friends call me Agan. At your service. I think Hypogeum is special to you. Regular tour, not enough. Special entrance for you."

"What do you mean?"

"For a price," he said, rubbing his fingers together to gesture money. "I show you where teacher and children were lost. First, we smoke some good shit, huh?"

This turn of events intrigued me, but I thought maybe this Agan saw me as a sucker tourist, could rob me or kill me or worse, and yet...

"How much?"

"Seventy-five American dollars," he said in a low voice. "I will show you things the tour guide never will."

"I can't afford it," I said. "I don't have much money."

The man stood up. For some reason, I stood up, too. I noticed that his back was bent and he had to look up at me, but his shoulders were like a linebacker. His leathery face grew thoughtful.

"For you, fifty dollars."

Chapter Nineteen

The Willies

I paid my tab at the Four Winds Pub and followed Agan out onto the street. At the end of the block, we turned down a dark side street. The alcohol must have given me stupid bravery.

We came to a basement entrance in the sidewalk, with a wrought iron fence to keep people from falling in, with stone steps going down below ground level. I saw other people going in and coming out, everyone in a festive mood. It seemed public and safe.

Agan turned to me.

"Is good time for fifty dollars."

I gave him two twenties and a ten.

We descended the stone steps and found a regular bar with pool tables, where people we had seen outside were playing pool. Agan led me past them to a heavy door, to which he had a key.

He unlocked the door and we entered a dark, smoky, low-ceilinged tavern. When my pupils adjusted I saw that the room was actually a cavern. A tavern in a cavern. The walls were unpainted limestone with irregular corners. Stalactites drooped from the ceiling. Some of the stalactites had strings of tiny lights wound around them, giving off eerie hues of color but not bright enough to light the room below. Near the middle of the room, a descending stalactite joined with a rising stalagmite, forming a narrow hourglass-shaped column. A shapely bare-bottomed server, carrying a tray of drinks, hung onto the hourglass column as she leaned into a turn. As she pivoted off the pole to change directions, I saw that all she wore was a small golden triangle in the front. She sashayed briskly and expertly in and out among the scattered patrons and tables. "Let's have a seat," said Agan at a corner table.

As soon as we sat down, a waiter placed two cups of coffee on our table and left without saying a word. An intoxicatingly delicious aroma of coffee and licorice warmed my sinuses when I held the cup near my face.

"Very good coffee," said Agan. "Freshly roasted, with chicory, cloves, and ground Aniseed."

"Aniseed," I remarked. "That's what absinthe and anise are made from. I drank anise in Spain."

"Yes, is good" he said as he loaded a long-stemmed pipe with hashish. He handed me the pipe and loaded another one for himself. The pipe stems were traditional sebsie, made with manual wood turning tools. The bowls were disposable clay.

Halfway across the room, another scantily clad server was bending over backwards as two men arm-wrestled on her stomach, as though she were a human table. That, I knew, was classic Dero activity. If one is to believe Richard Shaver, that server might have been a Dero captive.

We finished our coffee and pipes.

"You keep."

"Wow, thanks."

Agan stood up. I stood up and put the pipe in my pocket.

"We walk."

At the open end of the bar, a sign said Employees Only. Agan spoke to the bartender, who motioned for us to come in. Agan picked up a flashlight from under the bar and we went through a curtain of beads in the back wall, into a hallway of moist rock.

"Hypogeum," he said, somewhat dramatically I thought.

"Here?" I asked, feeling remarkably calm, clear-headed, and mood elevated. "But isn't the Hypogeum in Paola?"

"My friend," said Agan, "Hypogeum extends from one side of the island to other, and under the sea. Officials close most for safety. Normal tourist will never see. I tell you, no?"

Agan handed me the wide-beamed flashlight, the kind with a handle and a button for your thumb. The "hallway" was a rock corridor. It branched into two rock corridors.

At the end of the left corridor, a room as big as a house. My flashlight beam found a ten-foot-high wall, painted like the burnished cross-section of a Richard Shaver rock book. The overall design of the artwork was wavelike, as though someone had drawn a ten foot checkerboard, with squares of reddish-orange, brown, and plum, and then stretched the squares unevenly, creating an endless variety of four-corner angles, in relation to their location along a shifting tectonic taffy plates. I backed up, looked around, Agan was gone.

The wall from this distance looked like headlights were on.

Road map, time-lapse, streaking headlight photographs, nighttime turnpike cloverleaf, glistening bright city lights, take the exit feeling right. A feeling of well-being. I've returned here many times, sometimes asleep.

I walk into the little shop and see a black wrought-iron lamp, a smiling half-moon face halfway up the base like Mr. Midnight of the lampshade Zodiac, and cedar boxes with camphor bouquet, gemstones, meerschaum pipes, one-of-a-kind carvings of teakwood on necklace chains, and in the next room were black light posters, incense, clove cigarettes, patchouli oil. A curious puzzle box.

This whole block is like a honeycombed puzzle box. Many of these distinctly individual storefronts are connected in back. People back here had one chest of drawers on top of another, with a blanket hanging like a curtain where they go to get high then walk up some stairs to the roof, see the real moon, the fire escape steps to the alley, shot of vodka from my flask, walk out onto the sidewalk and look up at the great span of bridge overhead, gold-silver guardrail fins on lofty cloverleaf UFO with blinking bright night city lights, green traffic signs radiating for various exits.

The Starlight Café beckons from across the street. Beer, local painters on the wall, talk to John the owner, head down to another Mediterranean port. Dockside buildings always have those rusted steps up the outside wall. Inside, "what seasoned yeoman taped this defunct hand-written directory to the metal desk slide-out over the top left drawer?"

Shore leave, the Sangria Shack, Benny's Bar, in through the one door, out through the ferry that takes you to Tangier, Morocco, where the guide hustles you downstairs to a shop-within-a-shop, and everything glitters – fine silk tapestries, shiny medallions, enormous brass plates and shields, etched sapphire, turquoise jewelry, "four rays," referring to the four lines from each vertex to other vertices. This relates to the fourth-dimension tetra cube but I don't have much money so I keep reminding myself, "All that glitters is not necessary."

I took a page from Corpsman Jim's textbook about the four lobes of the brain, and a page from the Book of Ezekiel in the *Bible* describing the four walls of the Temple in the Old Testament. I cut up the pages and rearranged them into this poem:

> Idols of the injury,
> dug in behind the least understood
> motor plan information.
> The vile abomination temporal lobes and
> The four loathsome memory walls and
> The four reasoning, arithmetic beasts
> are found for all behind pain and planes.
> Portrayed as a house,
> Go in, function, cause blindness from
> The house's hearing spirit, judgment and
> The court's four bronze woes and
> The functioning brain lobe wings,
> Go in, hearing and perception,
> I dig under door fronts, pain and plans.

My grandparents had a grandfather clock, rococo furniture, fireplace, staircase climbing into the unknown. It reminded me of *The Bat* (1959). One night in near darkness, while the grownups played cards downstairs, I went upstairs find cloth in my grandmother's sewing room to make a Lee Falk Phantom mask. What I thought it was the door to the sewing room was a fourth room, colder than anywhere else in the house. I bumped into a ladder that led up to the attic, so I climbed. In the attic, my cousin, Harry and his friend Rudy, both Viet Nam Veterans, drinking and smoking. On a wooden box crate sat half a bottle of whiskey, cigarettes, a small battery lamp, and a barely audible transistor radio. There were no other lights in the room.

"You found our hiding place," said Harry.

"Have a drink," said Rudy, handing me the bottle.

I was just a kid, but I took a drink from the bottle. The whiskey was nasty and harsh going down, but it produced a golden glow of well-being. In that instant, I understood why people like booze.

"Want a cigarette?" asked Rudy.

"Don't give him no cigarette, asshole," said Harry, taking the bottle from me and gulping down a swig. Rudy sat down cross-legged on the floor, rocking back and forth to the barely audible radio music, grinning drunk and says to me, "You want to get the willies?"

Harry stood up, lit a cigarette. "He might rat us out."

"Let's give him the willies!" said Rudy.

"What are you talking about?" I asked. "I won't rat you out."

"Grimm's Tale," said Rudy, "about a boy wants to learn what fear feels like. The Sexton says I'll give you the willies! Three nights in a haunted house and *death walks tonight!*"

Harry handed me the whiskey and said, "You gonna need more of this."

Rudy shined the light on an old storage trunk. Now the whiskey didn't burn so much. It tasted good. I opened the trunk. Inside was a mummified human skeleton in a long, billowy dress. The dress was yellow from age. Long white hair hung from the dried-up scalp. Some of the joints had been wired together. Rudy handed me the light and said, "Operate the spotlight, boy!"

I swear the skeleton stood without any help. One hand steadied on the edge of the trunk. The skeleton stretched out its other arm and Rudy scooped it into his arms. They moved like ballroom dancers. I followed them with the spotlight. Monstrous vaulted shadows swayed from one extreme angle to…

"Cut in!" said Rudy.

He handed the skeleton off to me and my right eye looking into hers. With a hoarse gurgle the skeleton spewed green orbs from its mouth, all over me like slick marbles.

I must have blinked because I was still in the Hypogeum and heat was coming off the wall.

Prism pigment caterpillars writhed and dropped off the wall from the heat radiating from the other side. The wall got hotter, brighter, and bulging like a bubble. The bubble popped, I felt spray and rivulets of lava poured down and the hole grew larger, until the hole became an opening. I saw a green man with arms like a praying mantis, wearing animal skin. I couldn't run because hardened lava encased my feet.

The green humanoid stepped through the opening. One insect arm stretched out beside my head. The first joint closed on my head with those spiney barbs cutting into my face. I felt the other arm clamping around my ankles. The hardened lava around my feet cracked as the green humanoid lifted me up over its head. I thought it was going to throw me against the wall, but the arm around my head had loosened and cradled my neck. I rolled my head weakly, taking in the surroundings.

Chapter Twenty

Lager and Coffee

The humanoid carried me further into darkness. I looked down from where it held me over its head and saw rows of rock slabs where stacked mummified remains moaned or whistled. We passed by a slab that held nothing but the small skeletons of children. Their teacher wrapped her wispy arms around them, dissolved like smoke, reappeared and did it again and again.

I turned my head and squinted at an ancient bronze medallion on the mutant's chest. A four-pointed star. Directly under the star symbol, the depiction of a snake or serpent. A sparkling rainbow danced upon the scales of the raised bronze serpent as it writhed to free itself from the medallion. Revulsion consumed me when the hideous worm dropped from its mount and landed on my chest. I brushed it away, but when I looked back at the medallion, another snake emerged sideways from a fissure in the bronze, writhing, pulsating, shedding under the ancient graven star.

A cold sprinkle of water on my forehead startled me.

As with all galaxies, elements are released from the first star when it explodes into a supernova.

The water felt good. I looked. The snake no longer moved.

I was looking at a bronze medal on Roger's green Army uniform. The "snake" under the actual four-pointed star was a wreath of olive branches.

Roger's kind eyes watched me attentively from beneath his Army cap. Poised to sprinkle more water on my face, he stopped when he saw me looking at the object pinned to his chest.

"You like my new medal?" he said. "It's a NATO medal. I got it in Sigonella."

"You're not a Dero," I said.

"You thought I was a Dero?" he asked. "No, man, but I had to pay a leprechaun twenty bucks to tell me where you were."

"You . . . oh, really?" I said. "You got off cheap."

"You should drink a lot of water. I have two canteens full."

He handed me a canteen and I drank.

Roger had a lantern-style flashlight even brighter than mine sitting the ground. He picked up my flashlight and it still worked.

I noticed a 35mm camera on a strap hanging by his side.

"You brought a camera?"

"Oh, shit yeah, I got photos galore for the *Beat.*"

Sitting up I said, "Man, I'm so glad you brought a camera!"

"Of course," he said, helping me up.

"I must have been tripping my balls off."

"Did you do that?" asked Roger, pointing high up on the wall, higher than anyone could reach without a ladder. Silver and luminous in the flashlight beam were the initials "P.C."

"What the hell?" I said. "Did you do that?"

"I just asked you if you did it! I swear I didn't. How could I?"

"How could I?"

"With a ladder?"

"Neither one of us is even close to having a ladder. That's got to be a coincidence."

"Yeah, nothing related to Paul. But I'll take a couple of pictures, just in case."

We walked back through the cavern tavern. It was empty except for a lone bored bartender, who, without a word, let us out and locked the door behind us like it happened every day. Roger and I walked up the steps and emerged into the morning light on the side street.

Back at the hotel, I showered and slept for two hours. Roger woke me up. I showered again and put on clean clothes. We joined Craig and Nancy for brunch at an outdoor café connected to the hotel.

I sat down and asked the server for a Farson Cisk Lager and a cup of espresso, explaining, "I'm kind of tired but I still need something to take the edge off."

Craig smiled at that. He ordered coffee. He had a book with him, so I asked him about it and we talked.

Roger had changed out of his uniform, into his white buckskin vest with western tassels. His hair was cut short, Army style. He pulled a cheroot from his leather cartridge pouch and fired it up. He too enjoyed a cold bottle of Farson Cisk Lager.

Nancy said, "Whit, we were so worried about you. Don't go off by yourself again. Stay with us. Nicolo is coming later to take us to the motor pool. To see this guy Clemens who works there."

"Clemens?"

"You were asleep."

"Let me fill you in," said Craig. "Whit, I like your *Astral Beat* venture. While you were asleep, Roger told me and Nancy about the P.C. initials. I realized, and I'm sure you know this, the most direct route to documenting the P.C. initials would be to ask the museum curators."

I couldn't believe I hadn't thought of it.

"Of course," I said. "Has anyone…"

"Yeah. I spoke to the head Curator this morning, who checked into it." Craig smiled and continued. "He said it was nothing more or less than graffiti vandalism. He thanked me for bringing it to his attention."

"Did you ask him how long it had been there?"

"I did. He said the room in question is seldom visited, and a work crew with a scaffold or ladder hasn't been in that area since before he became a curator."

"Top notch reporting," said Roger.

"There's one more thing," said Craig. "I had to call Nicolo to verify our next pick-up time. On a hunch, I asked him if knew the first name of the Clemens at the Motor Pool. He said no but we could probably meet him today."

A half hour later, we were passengers once again in Nicolo's efficient Renault taxi, briskly tooling along a stretch of road between Valletta and the airport.

With the addition of Roger to our party, Nancy sat tightly between Craig and me in the back seat, while Roger rode in the front passenger side, seat pushed back, knees against the dashboard.

The taxi station was a handsome stucco office building in front of a big parking lot surrounded by a chain link fence. Nicolo drove us through the wide-open gates, past some water-hose spray and flying soap suds where a young boy and girl were washing cabs. We rolled into a sizable garage full of open bay mechanic stations. The occasional whine of pneumatic wrenches and air compressors bounced off the walls.

We stopped near a hydraulic jack with a car in the air, a man in overalls standing under the car, tightening something.

"Young Clemens!" Nicolo gave a friendly shout.

"What's new, Mr. Nick?" the mechanic smiled, wiping his forehead with his sleeve, brushing unruly black hair out of his eyes.

He laid the wrench on a metal toolbox cabinet and approached us.

"Nothing new," said Nicolo. "Another day at the races!"

I rolled down the window in the back seat and said, "We're looking for Paul Clemens."

"Who?" asked the young man.

"But this is the fellow," said Nicolo. "This is young Clemens!"

It was not Paul Clemens.

To the young mechanic, Nicolo said, "My friends thought they might know you, but I didn't know your first name."

"Ralph Clemens," said the mechanic. "From Ohio. Never heard of Paul. Sorry."

I felt dizzy.

I woke up in my hotel bedroom. There was a skylight in the ceiling but I couldn't tell if it was dusk or dawn. A shaft of light caught my eye as the bedroom door opened quietly and a dark figure entered the room, accompanied by an alluring fragrance of bath product.

I turned on the lamp beside the bed. It was Nancy, with a towel around her head, wearing a soft white robe and a pair of rubber flip-flop sandals.

"I hope I didn't wake you up," she said. "You were exhausted, but I thought I should check on you."

"You're checking on me?"

"Yeah, Roger isn't telling us anything about what you and he saw underground. He says it's classified."

"Damn right it is."

"Goodnight Whit."

In the first edition of this book, I wrote that Nancy and I had sex at this juncture of the story. But we didn't, because we both knew it would not ring true.

Chapter Twenty-One

The Age of Reason

Back in Hansburg, the Olsen Archer interview looked great in print. The hypogeum story was harder to make sense of. I was feeling better. Carnes prescribed something.

Nancy and Craig were back at Hampton University and Roger was back at his job. Anne called me to say she had picked up Roger's pictures of Malta at the Photo-Mat. I jumped on my bike and pedaled over to the new subdivision near the mall, where Anne and Roger had bought a house.

"Hey, Tyler," I said.

Tyler looked up at me through the screen door, a Popsicle in his hand. Anne appeared behind the child, smiling.

"Look, Tyler," she said. "It's Whit. Come on in."

We sat at the kitchen table and opened the packet of photos.

"Oh, look!" I said. "He ordered doubles. There are two of each photo. Look at this one."

Roger had taken good pictures of the Hypogeum and several well-composed shots of Malta above ground, with Nancy, Craig, me, and our guide, Nicolo. Craig and Nancy had also taken turns with the camera so Roger could be included in a few shots, mostly in his Army uniform.

I said, "Roger looks sharp in his uniform, doesn't he?"

"Yeah, as long as he doesn't get paint on it."

"Paint?"

"Oh, yeah," she said. "He got some kind of silver paint on his sleeve. I don't think it's going to come out, either."

"How did he get paint on it?" I asked.

"Lord knows," she said with an amused shrug. "I haven't got the whole story from him yet. I think he and Tyler must compete to see who can get the most challenging stains."

"He was painting in his uniform? Was this after he got back from Malta?"

"No, it was already there when he got back. I figured it was some crazy thing you and he did."

Even as Anne said these words, I came to a photograph of the wall in the Hypogeum that bore the luminous silver initials "P.C."

"What? Are you okay?"

"Huh? Oh, sorry," I said. "These are really great pictures."

"Would you like something to drink? Iced tea?"

"Uh, no, thanks. I guess I should get back to my typewriter. How much do I owe you for these?"

"Oh, don't worry about it," she said. "Roger wants to contribute to the newspaper anyway."

I said goodbye to Anne and Tyler. Instead of going straight home, I rode the bicycle hard, thinking, "What kind of horse shit is that? If Roger painted those initials, he should have told me. Is he trying to make a fool of me?" You know how it is."

Chapter Twenty-Two

Telepathy

Rolling into my parents' driveway, I swung my leg off over the front of the bike, licked the stand with my other foot. Left the bike standing in front of the brick flowerbed. A butterfly flittered around blossoming snapdragons of candy-corn yellow, luminous orange, and mottled red, pink. My mother's flowers – always beautiful.

I sat on the edge of the flowerbed with my head drooping to my knees, tired. Wiping sweat off my face with the bottom of my t-shirt, I heard a buzzing sound. Bee? No, a muffled ringing from under the flowers. The hidden phone. Reaching carefully through the vigorous sweet-smelling snapdragons, I dug my hand into the dirt and lifted the lunchbox out, phone still ringing, I opened it with both hands and caught the phone when it fell out.

"Hello?"

"Hello, Whit?" came a voice from somewhere in the sky wires. "This is Paul Clemens. Man, I can't believe you answered!"

"Paul? Where you calling from?"

"I'm in Four Corners, Colorado, where four states come together in one place. Colorado, Utah, Arizona, and New Mexico. I'm on ancient Aztec land even as we speak!"

"Ancient Aztec? What are you doing there?"

"I'm a Park Ranger with the State Recreation Department. We moved up here years ago for my dad's health. I wrote a letter to my girlfriend, but she never wrote back so I went deep woods."

"I thought you wrote 'Four Winds' on the dome in the woods. Not Four Corners."

"I don't remember what I wrote."

"Oh."

"Well, look, I didn't really expect you to answer, and I have to go, but we should talk again."

"Paul, before you go, I've got to know one thing. How did you sneak out from under those leaves?"

"Leaves?"

"Yeah, when we played kick the can! The last time I saw you, you were hiding under a pile of leaves!"

"Oh, right, I remember! Well, the trick was, I didn't actually hide in the leaves that time."

"But I saw you go under the pile!"

"No, you only thought you saw that. I stuck my arm into the leaves and looked at you, and you wedged yourself into your pile of leaves, and I hauled my ass home."

"And then moved away?"

"Yeah, pretty soon after that, we moved."

"Wow. It became the Paul Clemens the Boy who Hid in Leaves Mystery," I said.

"Great," said Paul. "That's a damn long-ass name but, so are you and Roger keeping the search alive?"

"What do you mean?"

"You know, the search for the unknown!"

"Well," I said. "I guess Roger is, anyway."

"Good old Roger!" said Paul Clemens. "Keeping the faith! Well, gotta go. Talk to you later."

"Okay, later."

I hung up the phone slowly and sat looking at it in wonder. Finally, I placed the phone back in the Johnny Quest lunchbox, closed the lid, put it back in the ground.

Good old Roger wasn't trying to make a fool of me. He painted those initials because he knew I needed a something, some focus maybe, I don't know. And he gave me plausible deniability by not telling me, so when I wrote the piece it would ring purely true. Paint on his sleeve. How did I miss that? Oh, right, tripping.

Chapter Twenty-Three

The Veiled Sons of the Valley

The next day I received a package from Craig. I pulled open the perforated edge of the manila envelope and tilted it. A shiny hardcover volume slid with a thump onto my desk, followed by a smaller book, which I recognized as my green diary. I must have left it at Hampton University or in Malta, and Craig or Nancy found it. I set the diary aside and looked at a hardcover book: *Haunted Mountains, Hidden Caverns* by Olsen Archer. I parted the crisp, new-book-scented pages and read Olsen Archer's Introduction:

> My collaboration with Richard Shaver ended sadly and abruptly when Mr. Shaver passed away on November 5, 1975. I am indebted to Mr. Shaver, not only for his published literature, which is now collectively referred to as the "Shaver Mystery," but also for granting me access to his collection of rock books, and for the fascinating conversations we shared.
>
> Mr. Shaver's rock books have been called "folk art" and "outsider art." In this book we will look at the rock books as cult art, pop art, and as one pillar of a triangular correlation between the Shaver Mystery, the Malta Hypogeum, and the

cavern networks of Appalachia. We will also examine synchronous connections with other underground, cavern-dwelling humanoids around the world.

Evil Scandinavian trolls, scuttling through rural towns at night to desecrate churches and steal babies from peat-roofed houses.

Scottish gnomes, who took refuge in caverns during the Dark Ages, to escape marauders, and left behind cave paintings and small quartz pebbles painted with symbols and wavy lines.

The Veiled Sons of the Valley, a family-owned network of caverns below the Appalachian Mountains, in the Shenandoah Valley. Records show the caverns were licensed for tours but never opened.

I turned to a chapter called "Under Appalachia" and read:

Along Interstate 81, in the foothills of the Appalachian Mountains, one 200 mile stretch alone boasts at least a dozen caverns that are open for guided tours. Most of these extend much further than the public will ever see. This is partly due to safety concerns, but also because it is not economical to survey a distance greater than the average tourist is willing to walk.

Endless Caverns in New Market, Virginia boasts "over five miles of caverns mapped with no end in sight."

The chambers of Luray Caverns, also in the Shenandoah Valley, are so irregular in shape that geologists have never measured them conclusively.

An especially strange story involves Four Chamber Caverns in the Shenandoah Valley, seven miles south of Hansburg, Virginia. In 1952, four brothers inherited one of the few gold mines in that part of Virginia from their mother, whose name was Shenandoah Drake. Shenandoah, incidentally, is a Native American term meaning "daughter of the stars."

A local Hansburg druggist claimed that on more than one occasion, two of the "Sons" as he called them, visited his pharmacy late at night, just before closing, to purchase paregoric. The druggist described them as stooped and strange in their old-fashioned Victorian frock coats. Most disconcerting of all, they wore black felt hats with dark veils, as were generally worn by old women in mourning. The first time this happened, the druggist thought he was being robbed, until one of the sons held forth a fifty-dollar bill and told him to keep the change.

Chapter Twenty-Four

The Lotus Blossom

I went to the kitchen and grabbed an apple from the fruit bowl, for fructose, and back to my room. I turned my attention to the faded green diary. The key was wedged under the strap. Something bulged inside, between the pages. I unlocked the strap and opened the book. A stiff square of folded wax paper dropped out, hit the desk vertically with a clack, and fell flat, the four-leaf clover pressed inside. I opened the diary wider and the four-picture strip of us in the photo booth fluttered down. An unfamiliar packet of folded paper fell out. It was a two by four-inch rectangle. I tried to unfold it. Little paper triangles popped up like a blooming lotus flower, crisp and timeless, self-illuminating glucose neon remembrance:

One day at school, in the fourth grade, Nancy and Anne made a couple of those origami fortune-tellers. Some kids call them cootie catchers. Open and closed, side to side, open, close, front to back. "Pick a color," Nancy had said. I saw blue, red, yellow, green. I said "Blue" and she said "B, L, U, E," opening and closing halves of the fortune-teller, side to side and front to back. "Now pick a number." "Three," I said. "One, two, three," she lifted the flap and read, "You will have a great adventure."

"Do it again!" I couldn't get enough of it. One, two, I would become an astronaut. Five, six, I would marry a toad. Eight, nine, I had ants in my pants. When I lost myself in the soothing mechanics of Nancy's paper flower, confidently manipulated by her feminine little fingers, I was in a safe world. I tried to make a cootie catcher with regular loose-leaf notebook paper but couldn't figure out the folds. "Would you make me one?" I asked Nancy. "Okay," but she never got around to it. Now, all these years later, Nancy had carefully torn a page from my diary, trimmed it square, and made an cootie catcher for me. I smiled and lifted one of the flaps. My own handwriting spelled out East, Downtown, Summer. I lifted another flap. My handwriting said South, Leaves, Autumn.

Now, this is interesting, I thought. The flap marked "8" opens to yellow, which opens to summer down Main Street. But open and close the fortune teller, this way and that, and you fold open sledding down danger hill, overlap blue winter static wool spark in the back seat. My favorite pages, before I learned how to read, were in *A Child's Encyclopedia of Science*. It started with a skeleton. When you turned a clear plastic page over the skeleton, you saw the heart, lungs, and guts in color. Flip another page and see veins and nerves. Unresolved slices of life when viewed separately, almost too painful to revisit. But live each day connected with all the other days and nothing is lost.

Olsen Archer's references to the Caverns of Appalachia and the Veiled Sons of the Valley have renewed my enthusiasm for "my own back yard," so to speak. I look out my bedroom window at night and see bats flying around the streetlight on the corner. Cars meet side by side under the streetlight then take off in opposite directions. Could be illegal rally racing, I don't know. An obituary said someone connected with the Veiled Sons died homeless, which I thought was an appalling thing for an obit to include, but what do I know?

Roger envisions an *Astral Beat* anthology in the bookstore at the Olsen Archer Museum. He is acting as my literary agent and sending inquiry letters to publishers. But I don't know.

Nancy wrote me a letter to say that Craig has asked her to marry him, but she told him she didn't even want to think about marriage until she finished college and started a career. I haven't answered her back yet. I need to thank Craig for sending his father's book.

Will I ever be ready for marriage? I don't know.

What will I do when the Hypogeum story is finished? I don't know.

Roger and Anne are having another kid. Will I ever be ready to have a kid? I don't know. There is still so much that I just don't know. Most of the time, I sit in my room, looking out my window with darkness-absorbing night pupils, hands together under the origami lotus fortune-teller. I manipulate the four paper diamonds with my thumbs and forefingers, open, closed, side-to-side, front-to-back, open, closed, watching the chapters of my life converge and scatter, converge and scatter.

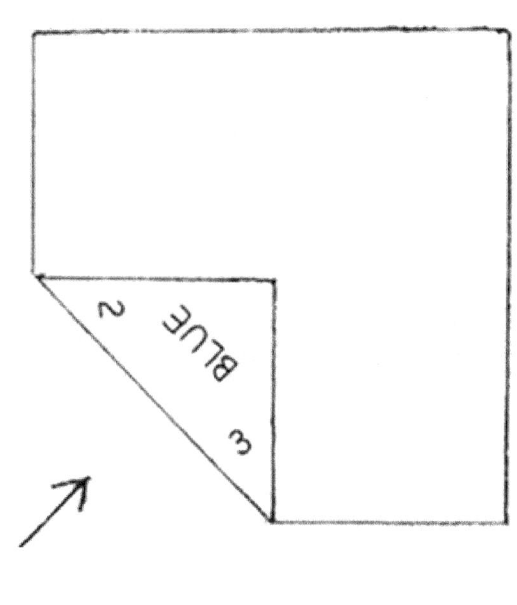
2
BLUE
3

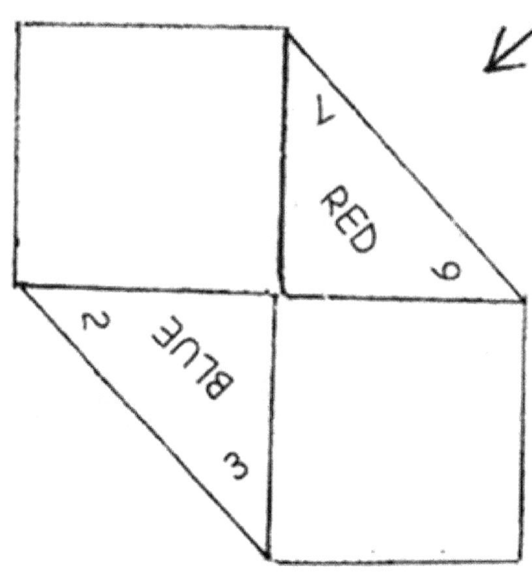
7
RED
6
2
BLUE
3

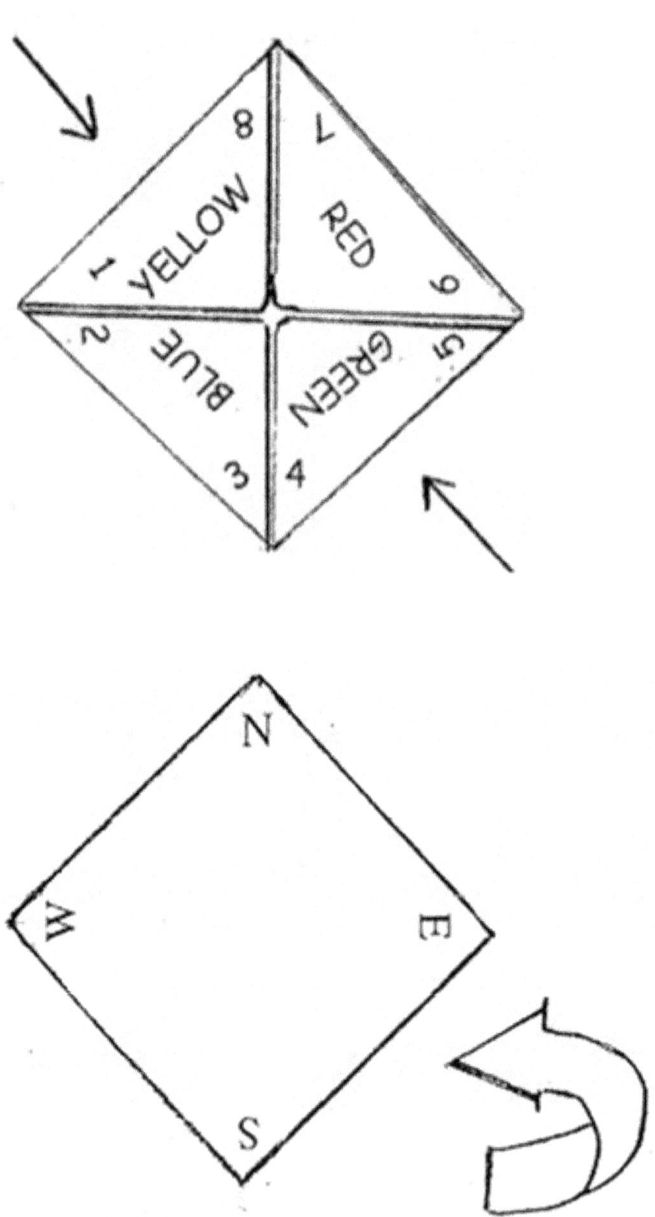
8
7
YELLOW
RED
1
6
2
5
BLUE
GREEN
3
4
N
W
E
S

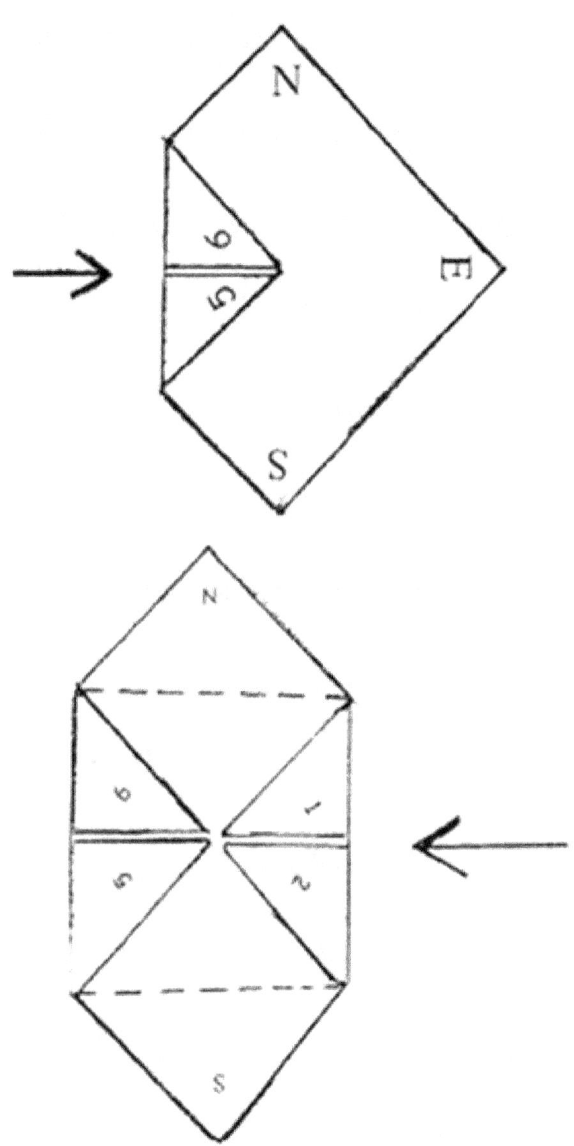
N
E
S
6
5
N
1
6
2
5
S

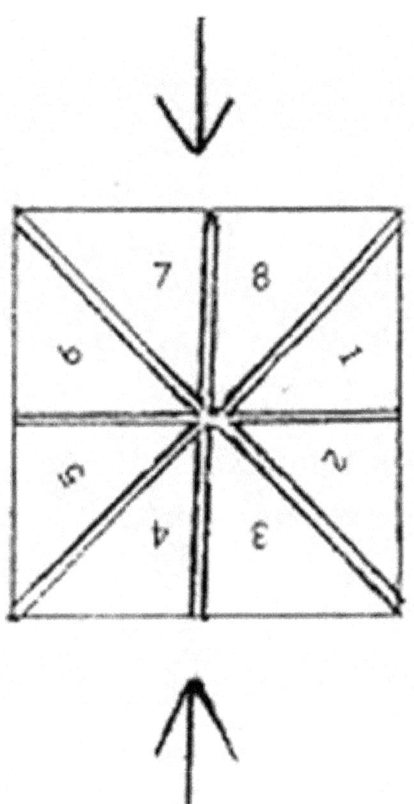
7
8
6
1
5
2
4
3

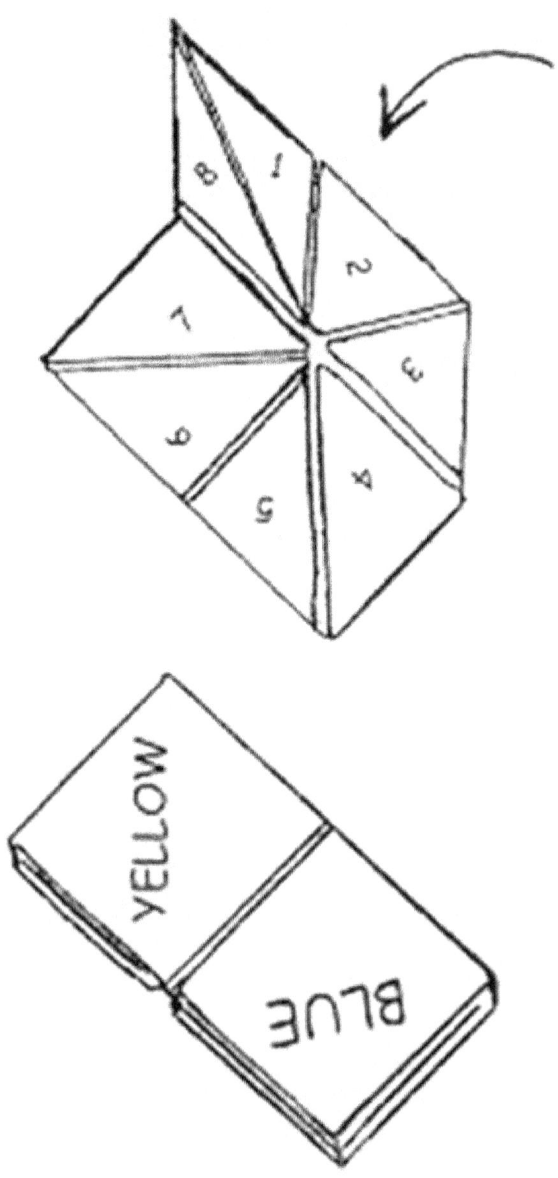
8
1
7
2
6
3
5
4
YELLOW
BLUE

YELLOW
UE
3
4
RE
YELLOW

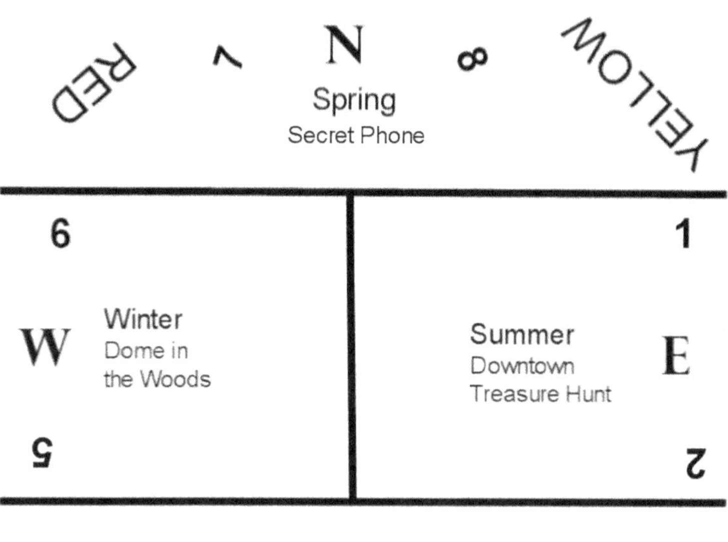

RED
7
N
8
YELLOW
Spring
Secret Phone
6
1
W
Winter
Dome in
the Woods
Summer
Downtown
Treasure Hunt
E
5
2

Fall
Buried Under Leaves
GREEN
4
S
3
BLUE

Thank you for reading *Tamper*.

billectric.com

9 798218 744847